T0114988

WOUNDED IN DARKNESS, HEALED IN THE LIGHT

LaTonya G. Green

authorHOUSE®

AuthorHouse™
1663 Liberty Drive
Bloomington, IN 47403
www.authorhouse.com
Phone: 1-800-839-8640

First published by AuthorHouse 03/21/2011

ISBN: 978-1-4567-3786-3 (sc)
ISBN: 978-1-4567-3785-6 (e-b)

Library of Congress Control Number: 2011902853
Cover Design by Ananiy Vasyura & LaTonya G. Green
Printed in the United States of America

While this book is based on a true story, character names and places in this book are used fictitiously and are a product of the author's imagination.

References to God, Jesus, the Holy Spirit and the Holy Bible are not fictitious.

Scripture quotations marked "KJV" are taken from the Holy Bible, King James Version.

Scripture quotations marked "NLT" are taken from the Holy Bible, New Living Translation Version.

Foreword

The Inspiration of a Winner!

Being a three time national championship title winner at the University of Miami has afforded me the privilege of being around some great players and great people and one thing you begin to notice about a great one, is that you can never tell when they have been through something unless they show you their scars and in this book, that is just what LaTonya G. Green has done. She has decided to show us her scars on her way to victory to prove that overcoming life's challenges are the result of a string of decisions to win on purpose.

When I LaTonya and her husband Mark, she had come to speak to our congregation. She had just returned from a mission trip to Uganda and she seemed to be a nice young lady, and when she spoke, you could tell that it was going to be inspiring.

I believe that this book is a winner and I believe it

is going to reveal some of your hidden scars that you can address. However, I also believe that this book is going to inspire you. My prophetic word to you is that as you read this book, you will refer it to someone else that needs to know that they are a decision away from victory. Additionally, I believe that you will enjoy the second book that is to come in this series as much as you are touched by LaTonya's inspiration to win in life from this one.

Pastor Derrick Golden
The New Covenant Fellowship Church of McKinney, TX

Special Thanks Go To:

First and foremost, I thank God, who made what seemed impossible possible and allowed this book to go from being a vision to a reality. I can do all things thru Christ Jesus who strengthens me!

Mark Anthony Green, my wonderful husband and best friend. Thank you for loving me and encouraging me to go beyond where I am and for believing in me. You are my #1 fan and I love you!

Bisola Ogunmola, my personal editor and dear friend, who worked diligently on this project as if it were her own. Thank you for pushing me to finish when I wanted to quit. Much love to you!

My children: Christopher, Jessica, Tashema, Briauna and Aaliyah. Keep God first, dream big dreams and then work hard to make them come true. I love you all.

My mom: without you, there would be no me. I love you.

Pastors Derrick and Ilya Golden, who embrace the anointing on my life and want to expose it to the world. We will turn the world upside down!

Last but not least, all those who cheered me on until the last word of this book was written.

Thank you, Thank you, Thank you!

About the Cover

On the front cover, there are three silhouettes. The first and smallest is a full bodied silhouette, completely black. This represents when our lives are filled with various components of darkness. This may be sin, bitterness, unforgiveness, old wounds that still hurt and things of that nature.

You will notice the silhouette is heading towards the light. When we decide to turn our lives over to Christ, we are drawn into His light. After we have accepted Christ, a transformation begins to happen in us.

The second silhouette, the one in the middle, is now starting to be embodied with light. During the transformation process, we are able to cast our cares on God who cares for us. As we do this, He takes our burdens which are heavy and gives us His burdens which are light. Once this happens, we can begin to raise our hands in worship as you see the silhouette doing.

The third and largest silhouette has some light and dark places. Once in Christ, His light is transforming us but it does not happen all at once. This silhouette also has an outline of light around the outside of it. This represents when the transformation is happening on the inside, there is a change on the outside that others can now see. Our light is now shining for the entire world to see and it will continue to get brighter and brighter as the healing continues!

Additionally, on the outside of the third silhouette, you will see that it has light and darkness surrounding it. Before Christ, the silhouette was completely surrounded by darkness. Once the light of Christ shows up, darkness has to flee. The darkness is now shrinking back as the light overtakes it.

Lastly, there are some different sized chains that are going through the silhouettes. These chains represent the issues that keep us in bondage. Some are small issues and some are big issues, but they all keep us bound. Some are small things and some are big things, but they all keep us bound. When we take them to God, at the point they connect with the light, they are broken. Notice that at each point a chain meets the light, it is broken. This is how we get liberty in Christ. He breaks the chains and sets the captives free!

On the back cover, the silhouette is present without any darkness. This represents a life that is fully submitted to Christ.

MY NAME IS JOSETTE and my story began on a cold winter's day in Brownwood, Michigan. I was born to a sixteen year old girl named Angela. The earliest memory I have is of the day my little brother Shawn Jr. died. I was about three years old. We were waiting for Angela to take us somewhere as soon as she finished getting dressed. Shawn and I were already dressed and sitting on the living room couch.

There was a dry cleaner's bag laying on the couch. Shawn grabbed the plastic bag and began playing with it. Somehow he got the bag over his head. He was pretending like he was grabbing at me and we were both laughing. Suddenly, he stopped laughing but he was still acting like he was grabbing at me. I kept laughing because he looked really funny. He finally stopped grabbing at me and laid down on the couch. I thought he was tired of playing so I just sat back on the couch. Shawn went to sleep.

When Angela finally came out of the other

room and saw us, she started screaming. I did not know why she was screaming. She picked up Shawn and began to tear the plastic bag off him. She was shaking Shawn and calling his name. He did not wake up. I knew something was wrong, I just did not know what it was. That was the last day I played with Shawn. When I asked where he was, the only answer I ever got was that he was gone.

After that, I was sent to live with my grandma after Shawn left. I did not know it at the time, but she was not my real grandma. Angela had spent most of her life in foster care and had suffered much abuse during those years. When she was fifteen, Angela was sent to live with Grandma. She was Angela's foster mother, but she was the only grandma I knew.

Grandma also had other foster children. They all called her Momma. When Angela left me with her, I began to call her Momma also. When she came back to get me, I started calling her Angela. She did not like it and told me that she was my momma and that I was to call her that. I did not want to, so I did not call her anything. She had been gone so long; it felt like Grandma was my mother. I called her Momma to her face, but she would always be Angela to me.

While I was at Grandma's house, Angela had gotten married to Shawn Jr.'s dad and she had given birth to a set of twin boys, Brandon and Brian. I was excited to go so that I could play with my new little brothers.

When I got there, it was not at all what I expected. My stepdad was really mean to me. He did not want me to go near the boys. He would yell at me and make scary faces when Angela was not paying attention. I tried to be good, but it seemed like I got in trouble for everything I did.

One night, I heard Angela and him arguing about me. He said he did not want me there. I heard him telling Angela that he thought it was just going to be him, her and the boys. I hated it there and wanted to go back to Grandma's house. Apparently, Shawn got his way because I was taken back to Grandma's house.

Angela finally came back to get me when it was time for me to start kindergarten. She had moved into the projects and Shawn was no longer around. Angela had a new boyfriend named Larry. I liked him because he was funny and treated her nice.

Larry owned a motorcycle. That was the first time I actually knew somebody that rode a motorcycle. He and Angela had a baby boy named Joseph. Life in the projects was not that bad in the beginning. I made friends, Larry liked me and I had three little brothers.

Angela took me to school and enrolled me in kindergarten. I was excited and ready to start school. I already knew how to read because I loved books and my older cousin Vickie had taught me how to read while I was at Grandma's.

IT WAS FINALLY THE first day of school. The hallways were long and wide. The floors were shiny and dark brown. There were kids everywhere. The classrooms had small wooden chairs pulled up to small tables. There were colorful drawings and alphabet letters pinned up on the walls. I walked around the room taking it all in.

Kindergarten classes only went half-days, so the first couple of days Angela picked me up. After that, I walked home. There were plenty of other kids walking to the projects, so I was not alone nor afraid.

I was beginning to not like school. I could not do anything until the teacher said it was time. I had to wait to play or talk. I even had to ask to go to the bathroom. At home, I could do those things when I wanted to. I began to act really bad in school. I cried, I talked back or would keep walking around when I was supposed to be sitting down. Sometimes I would be mean to the other kids by kicking or pinching them. They had not done anything to me, but it was the way I treated my brothers, so I felt okay treating the kids at school the same way.

The teacher talked to me every day about my behavior. When that did not seem to help, she began to call Angela. Every day I got home from school, I thought I would be in trouble, but Angela never said anything except that I had better be good in school. Her threats did not help because when I would go back to school I continued to do the same things.

One particular day, the teacher spanked me with her ruler and told me to sit down. I did not cry but it made me really mad. On the way back to my seat, I took some marbles from the play area. After I sat down, I put them in my mouth.

At first, the teacher did not know that I had them in my mouth, until she called my name and I did not answer. She called my name again and I just looked at her. It was then that she noticed that I had something in my mouth. She came over to me and told me to spit it out. Of course, I did not. After many attempts, she stopped trying. She left the room for a little while, then came back and continued teaching. I held those marbles tight in my mouth. I had shown her for spanking me!

The next thing I knew, Angela entered the room. She came right to me and grabbed my face and told me to spit out whatever I had in my mouth. She was squeezing my jaws so hard that I had no choice but to do it. Out came the marbles, rolling all over the floor. After they were out of my mouth, she took me to the front of the room and spanked me right in front of the rest of the class. The teacher did not have any more problems out of me from that day onward.

That year when Christmas came, Angela put up a Christmas tree. My brothers and I were very excited. There were not many presents under the tree, but we were happy that there were any at all. On Christmas day, we got to open our gifts. There was one gift for each of us. Mine was a big, beautiful baby doll. She was so pretty. She had long, pretty black hair with spiral curls on the end. She was wearing a pink and white dress with a matching bonnet with little white socks and shoes. I walked around holding her all day.

Later that day, Larry brought his daughter over to visit. Angela felt bad that she did not have a gift for her. She told me she was going to give her the doll and then get me another one just like it. I did not want to give it to her but Angela said we should be nice and think about other people. She then promised again that I would get another doll. I reluctantly gave her the doll.

I had to sit and watch her play with my doll for the rest of the evening. I bet she had a lot of Christmas presents at her house. Why did I have to give her my only present? After Christmas had come and gone, I never got the replacement doll that Angela had promised me.

ONE SUMMER DAY, LARRY had a motorcycle accident and he was killed. He had been riding my brother Joseph around that day. Right before the accident, he had let Joseph off the motorcycle and then was hit by a car. Good thing he did, or else Joseph probably would have been killed also. I guess Angela was too sad to take care of me, because I went back to Grandma's house for a little while.

She came and got me when it was time for school to start. We were still living in the projects but Joseph was not there when I got back. He had been taken by Larry's sister to live with her.

Eventually, Angela got a new boyfriend. His name was Derek. He was a big and tall man. He had a rough looking beard and mustache and was light-skinned. He smoked all the time. He was not mean to me but he did not really say much to me either. My brothers and I mostly stayed in our rooms when he was around.

At first, he only came by a little bit, and then

he began to be there every day. He and Angela seemed to sleep almost all the time. His everyday presence would be my first introduction to seeing drugs. I did not know it at first but later learned that Derek was a drug dealer. I mean the heavy stuff, heroin.

After a while, Derek moved in with us. I began to see needles and burnt spoons and small pieces of aluminum foil on the table all the time. One day, by accident, I saw Angela take a scarf and tie it around her arm and then take one of the needles and stick it in her arm. Almost immediately, she began falling asleep. She did not even take the needle out of her arm. I went back to my room because I did not want to get in trouble.

Not too long after that, Angela was not around that much anymore and she bought very little food for us to eat. She was always mad unless Derek was around. I began to steal food when we had it in the house because I did not know when we would get some again. I would sneak into the refrigerator at night and eat mayonnaise straight from the jar. I would hide cans of pork and beans and eat them in my room and throw the empty cans out the window.

It never dawned on me that someone would find the cans and just look up to know where they came from because the buildings were only two stories high. I looked forward to going to school now because I knew I would get to eat lunch. Life in the projects was no longer good.

The twins and I seemed to stay in trouble. Mostly me, because Angela said I should be watching them because I was the oldest. They were always doing something. Pulling stuff out of cabinets, making a mess all over the house. One night, they spilled a whole bag of rice on the kitchen floor and I had to clean it up. They never had to clean up anything.

I also had good times with them. We would make up games to play. We had bunk beds in our room, and one day while we were home alone, I decided that we were going to play like the beds were a school bus. I was the driver and they were my passengers. I stuck a bobby pin in the electric socket that was next to the bed so I could start the bus. As soon as I put it in the plug, there was a spark and a noise, and then all the lights went out. When I looked at the wall, it had black stuff all around the socket.

I did not know that I was not supposed to put objects in it and could have killed myself. When Angela came home, she did not know why the lights would not come on, and we did not tell her.

I had cleaned the black stuff off the wall, so she never knew what happened.

Angela was pregnant again, so we moved out of the projects into a big white house. It had a living room, dining room, kitchen, two bedrooms downstairs, a big room upstairs and a basement. It also had a fenced-in back yard. It was bigger than Grandma's house.

Angela got us a dog. It was a brown and white St. Bernard. He reminded me of the St. Bernard dogs I had read about. The only thing he was missing was the little barrel strapped around his neck. He was big, but he was gentle. We kept him in the basement except for when we let him out into the backyard.

We didn't have him long before he got sick and died. Angela and I put him in a large black garbage bag and put his body out for pickup with the rest of the trash. I thought maybe I would be sad, but I felt absolutely nothing while we were doing it.

There were always guns and drugs laying on the dining room table. We had been told not to ever touch anything on the table, so we never did. Angela was high every day. There were people in and out of the house all the time. My brothers and I were not able to make friends. The kids on the block called us the crack house kids. It didn't matter to us because we were used to playing with each other anyway.

My brothers and I would to go to the corner store and steal candy bars, chips and whatever else we could get our hands on. We would bring it home and make it our dinner. We got really good at it and began to do it almost every day. When one of my brothers got caught, we had to switch to another neighborhood store. The storekeeper told us we could not come into the store anymore but did not call the police.

We were scared after that, so we knew we had to be more careful. We did not stop stealing because it was still a way for us to get something to eat. On the day that my brother got caught, we went hungry that evening. We had learned how to drink a lot of water so that we would feel full before we went to bed. Sometimes I would lie in bed at night and listen to the water roll around in my stomach until I went to sleep.

One day when we came home from school, the lights would not come on. Angela did not come home that night, so we were there in the dark all night. The next day, when Angela came home, we told her the lights would not come on. She left and went next door to our neighbor's house. The next thing we knew, she came back and went into the back bedroom and opened the window. The neighbor threw a long orange extension cord over to her. She plugged it into a lamp and turned it on. She had brought us some food from somewhere, so we got to eat a meal that night. She went to sleep on the couch while we ate.

We shared electricity with the neighbor for about a week. Most nights, as usual, Angela was not there. Each night after it had been dark for awhile, the lamp would go off. We did not have a bedtime, but it was too dark for us to do anything, so we would go to bed when the lamp went off. We were so happy when our own lights came back on. We did not have to crowd around the lamp at night anymore. I was happy, because it was pretty spooky in the house at night when the lamp went out, even though I never told the twins that I felt that way. I had to be brave for them. The babies did not know the difference one way or the other.

Angela had been gone for three days and once again, there was nothing to eat. I decided to call Grandma and ask her if she would bring us some food. Grandma did not hesitate to say yes. When she came, she brought so many bags of food that we had to make several trips to the car to get it all out. I do not remember us ever having this much food at one time.

We were so excited and could not wait to eat it. It was all food that we could make ourselves. There was cereal and milk, pork and beans and hotdogs, bread, lunch meat, peanut butter and jelly. There were even some cookies! Grandma did not stay long, just long enough to get all the food inside.

Angela came home the next day. When she saw all the food, she asked where it came from. I told her Grandma brought it over. She called Grandma and asked her why she brought food when we did not need it. Grandma told her I had called because we were hungry. She told Angela she was just trying to help. Angela told her she did not need her help because she knew how to take care of her own kids.

She was so angry when she got off the phone. I already knew by the way the phone call went that I was going to get it. She called me out of the bedroom and asked why I called. I told her we were hungry and I did not know what else to do. She said she would teach me to tell other people her business.

Whenever we got whipped, it was with an extension cord and we had to take off all our clothes. She told me to go get the cord and take off my clothes. I think she whipped me as hard as she could that day. I finally fell on the floor and rolled into a ball. While I was lying on the floor, she took her foot and stomped my head into the floor several times. I thought I was going to die. It hurt so bad and there was nothing I could do. She finally stopped and told me to get up and go in my room.

I was sore and bleeding from the extension cord. I was not ever calling anybody else to ask for food. I would just keep stealing to avoid a beating like that again. That was the first day I felt hatred for Angela. She had never whipped me like that before.

IT HAD BEEN ANOTHER day of not eating. It was Saturday, so there was no school lunch to tide us over. Angela finally came home from wherever she had been. She had brought home a box of fried chicken from her favorite fast food restaurant. The only problem was that it was not a big box with enough chicken for all of us. It was a three piece snack sized box. Angela laid down on the couch and put the box on the floor next to the couch.

I was peeping out the bedroom door and watching her every move. She was not even thinking about feeding us or the fact that we had not eaten all day. She finally fell asleep. I told my brothers that I was going to get that chicken for us. I got a knife from the kitchen. I went into the living room, where she was still sleeping. I slowly and softly walked toward her. When I was directly over her, I looked at her lying on her back. I turned and saw my brothers watching me. I knew the only way I was going to get this chicken for us was to kill her.

I slowly raised the knife over my head with both my hands. I just stood there for a few moments, gathering up the courage to stab her. I held my breath and brought the knife down. I hit her chest and her eyes opened wide. I did not know that I would have to use more strength to actually stab and kill her. I just knew when she opened her eyes and I had not killed her that she was going to beat me crazy. But instead, she just stared at me. It was like she could not believe this was happening.

I dropped the knife, and the boys and I ran into the room. I waited because I knew that at any moment, she was going to call me out into the living room to beat me. When she finally called me out of the room, she did not have the extension cord. She just looked at me and asked me why I tried to stab her. I told her I needed to feed me and the boys and that was the only way I knew to get the chicken for us.

She looked at me like I was crazy and gave me the chicken. My brothers and I ate the chicken. Once again, in my own way, I had provided for them. Angela never whipped me for trying to stab her. My instinct to survive had caused me to almost kill Angela.

ONE COLD AND WINTRY day, I was walking my twin brothers to school. There were not any other children out by the time we left home. Angela was not there to wake us up, to help us get cleaned up and dressed for school. Once again, I had to be the mother. In fact, the twins expected me to do it because I had been doing it for so long. The three of us left the house without breakfast, but we all knew we would be able to eat lunch at school, so nobody said anything about not eating.

It was not snowing, but it was very cold. The streets had frozen snow covering them. With every step we made, the snow made a crunching noise under our feet. We half walked and half slid down the streets. Even though it was bitterly cold, we still played along the way.

We did not go to the same school. The routine was that I would walk the twins part of the way to their school and then I would head off to my school. But this day was different than any other day. I had gotten a new pair of boots. I got them from a clothing program, but unlike other things I had received, these boots were not used.

The boots were made out of soft suede-like material. They were dark brown on the outside, with light brown laces. The inside was my favorite part. The boots had a light brown furry material on the inside. They were so beautiful, and I could not wait to put them on. I did not wear them to school. I wanted to wait and put them on there. I wanted to make sure that when I got to school they would still look brand new.

This was very important to me because the other children at school always teased me about my hair and clothes. They called me dirty, stinky and ugly. I knew I was ugly because no one ever told me I was cute or beautiful, like they did the babies. I tried to make my hair look like the other girls, but it was so hard to comb and would not lay down flat. I hated them all with their pretty clothes and nicely-combed hair.

I did not have any friends, but I just knew that once the other girls saw my pretty boots they would want to be friends with me. But I never made it to school that day.

After I parted ways with the twins, I headed off in the direction of my school. I had a notebook in one hand and my boots tied together by the laces and thrown over my shoulders. As I was walking, a red car pulled up right in front of me. A man was driving the car. He reached over to the passenger side and rolled down the window. He was looking at a piece of paper and asked me if I knew where some street was.

I could not understand what street he was asking about and told him I did not know what he was saying. The man opened the passenger door and told me to look at the paper. I leaned in towards the car to look at the paper and when I did, he pulled me in the car and took off.

He made me sit down on the floor of the passenger side of the car. He snatched my boots and notebook from me and threw them in the back seat. He told me to pull my hat over my head. I was scared and began to cry. The man smacked me on the top of my head and told me to shut up. I knew how to stop making noise while crying because of all the whippings with Angela. I had never been this scared in my entire life. I started to cry quietly again.

The car finally stopped. He reached inside my coat and stuck his hand down the front of my shirt. His hand was so cold that it felt like a piece of ice. He moved his hand around and then removed it. I was only nine and did not have breasts like some of the other girls at school. It must have made him mad because he yelled for me to shut up. I was crying uncontrollably now. I wanted to stop but I could not. I think it made him madder.

He unzipped his pants and kept trying to put my mouth on his privates. It smelled like pee. I kept crying and started coughing. He kept trying to force my mouth on him. He finally made me do it. But with all the crying, coughing and my runny nose, his mission was not getting accomplished.

He finally just put me out in the middle of nowhere. I did not care because I was just glad to be out of the car. He drove off really fast. I was still crying. Then I realized he did not give me back my brand new boots. I began to cry even harder.

The icy snow was no longer fun. The glare of the sun on the snow was blinding my eyes. I closed my coat up and began to walk. I had no clue where I was, but then I saw a building that looked like a school in the distance. I headed towards the building. It was so cold that the tears were freezing up on my face. My hands were burning. The twins and I had coats, but we did not have gloves, so we would put socks on our hands to keep them warm. The socks were not working now.

As I continued to walk, I saw a man and a woman walking together towards me. The woman had on a long black coat and a soft furry looking hat and the man had on a brown coat with a scarf around his neck. I knew they were cold also because they both had their hands in their pockets and their shoulders where hunched up. It looked like they were trying to snuggle as far down in their coats as they could go.

They saw me and came over to where I was. They wanted to know why I was crying and asked me why I was not in school. I told them that a man had taken me and dropped me off there. The couple told me they would take me where I would be safe. They took me to the building that I was headed to.

When we got inside, we went into an office and they told the people what I told them. They began to ask me questions. It seemed like they were asking them all at one time. Did the man hurt me? Did I know the man? Had I ever seen him before? Why did I go with him? What was my parents' phone number? Where did I live? Where did I go to school?

I was scared again because I knew I was in big trouble. I did not mean to go with the man, but no one had ever told me not to talk to strangers, so I was not scared when he approached me. A nice lady brought me some hot chocolate to help me warm up. It was so good. It had been a long time since I had hot chocolate.

After I calmed down, they started asking me questions again. I told them the man did not do anything to me except drive me around and that I was okay. I did not want to lie to the people, but I did not want them to know what happened to me either. I just could not bring myself to tell them.

They asked for my phone number and I lied again. I told them that I did not have a phone because I knew it was disconnected. I told them what school I went to and how old I was. They called my school and the police. The school gave them all the phone numbers they had on file. They could not reach Angela. They tried another number the school gave them; it was Grandma's. She answered. They told her what happened and asked her to come down.

When Grandma got there, she started asking me the same questions the other people asked her. I lied again and said the man did not touch me. They released me to Grandma. I told Grandma that I was supposed to get the twins from school. I did not realize that the school day had already ended.

Grandma went to the school, but all the children were gone, including the twins. She drove to my house and the twins were waiting in the cold on the porch. I unlocked the door and let them all in. Inside, the babies were crying. They were wet and hungry. Once again, Angela had not come home.

I told the twins to get some diapers. Grandma and I changed them. We dressed the babies and Grandma took all of us home with her. When we got to her house, she fed us. I was so happy to eat since I had missed lunch at school. As soon as the food hit the table, I gobbled it up. Grandma told me to stop eating my food that fast because I might get sick. I was not worried about getting sick. I just wanted to make sure I got to finish the food.

Grandma went in her bedroom and called her sister. I could hear her talking on the phone. She was telling her everything that happened that day. I was so glad I did not tell her how the man had touched me and what he made me do. A little while later, Grandma's sister showed up to help her with us.

When Angela finally showed up, Grandma told her she was not taking me. She said I would just wind up back there, anyway, so I might as well stay. Angela took everybody with her except me. I never went back to live with Angela again after that day.

Now that I lived with Grandma, I had a chance to meet the kids that lived on her street. All the other times that I had gone to her house, I didn't go outside to play. When the kids on Grandma's street started asking where my mother was, I told them that she was dead. I did not know why I said it; it just came out. It made it easier for me not to have to explain why she was never around. They never asked me about my father.

Since it was the middle of the school year, Grandma got me enrolled in school a couple of days after being there. I guess she was giving me time to get over the kidnapping. I hoped it would be different at that school.

On the first day at my new school, some of the girls started messing with me. Somebody sent me a note telling me the names of everybody that wanted to fight me. At lunch time, on the playground, they picked at me. Some of them bumped into me on purpose and others pushed me. I did not accept the challenge to fight. Even though the girls at my old school teased me, they never picked any fights with me. The only fights I ever had were with my brothers.

At the end of each school day, I would walk three blocks home. A group of girls followed me every day for a week and a half. They would push and shove me. I did not want to fight. I just wanted them to leave me alone. I was not messing with them; why were they messing with me?

Finally, one day as I was walking home and they were picking at me, I dropped my books and turned around. There was a whole group of them and just one of me. I was scared but I was not going to act like I was scared. I asked who wanted to fight me, and the girl that had been causing me the most grief stepped forward. Her hair was parted straight down the middle, with two long braided pony tails that went past her shoulders. I was sure without question that she weighed more than me, because I was tall and bony.

When she stepped forward, the other girls circled us. She made the first move. She pushed me backwards. I stumbled but did not fall. I reached towards her and grabbed both of those braids. With one braid in each hand, I began to swing her around. I kept swinging until I could not keep her lifted anymore. I did not even know

I had that much strength. When I let her go, she hit the ground hard. I think I shocked everybody, including myself. I asked if there was anybody else who wanted to fight me and they all said no.

From that day forward, the girls no longer bothered me. Most of them became my friends. I had more fights, but those were with some of the girls on my street that were not in my class. I realized fighting was somewhat of a pastime on my street.

A fight would happen whenever somebody would tell one person they wanted to fight, and somehow the other person always found out. After that we would schedule the fights, almost like a professional boxing match. Both people would have the day and time, and all the other kids on the street who knew about it would show up to watch.

ANGELA WAS COMING TO pick me up so I could get my hair done for Easter. I was excited to go, but I pretended like I did not care. It really meant a lot to me. I still got teased at school because I had not been taught how to properly take care of my hair, so it was always nappy and not neatly combed.

Angela's picking me up was probably a nice little break for Grandma, due to the fact that I was a handful with my constant lying and stealing. I had not given up my way of survival. The only difference was that most of the things I stole were from Grandma's purse and the kitchen. I did not go to the stores in her neighborhood to steal.

When she got there, she told Grandma that she was going to buy me a new outfit. We left and went to one of her friend's house where there were other people waiting to get their hair done also. After we had been there for a while, Angela called me into the bathroom. She asked me what I had done with her hundred dollars and said to give it back. I did not know what she was talking about. Here we were in a house full of people, and she was only asking me about her missing money. These people probably used drugs just like her and one of them probably took the money.

I told her I did not have her money. She told me I was lying. I yelled really loud at her and told her she did not even know me. I told her I did not steal anymore, but she would not know that because she had not been around. The next thing I know, she slapped me so hard that my lip started bleeding. I hated her! I hated her! I hated her!

My eyes welled up with tears but I refused to cry. I tried to act like it did not hurt. She asked me again where the money was and I told her again that I did not have it. She called me a liar and a thief and left out of the bathroom. Who was she to talk? I had heard about all the times when Grandma said that Angela had stolen money from her, so how could she call me a thief?

I stayed in the bathroom until someone knocked on the door and said they needed to use it. I went back out in the living room. Finally the lady said she was ready for me, but I told her I did not want her to do my hair. I really did want my hair done, but I did not get it done because at that moment I did not want anything from Angela.

Angela glared at me like she wanted to kill me. I just sat there looking at her. I hoped she could hear me saying in my head how much I hated her. For whatever reason, she did not make me sit in the chair to get my hair done.

Before Angela took me back to Grandma's house, we stopped by another lady's house. That was where I was getting my Easter outfit from. We went down into the basement. There were racks and racks of clothes, just like in a store. The lady was a booster, which is a person who steals clothes or whatever else they can get from a store and then sell it to other people. Angela told me to look around and see if I saw anything I liked. I shopped around until I found a lavender skirt with a matching jacket. Angela picked something out for herself and paid for both outfits. She then drove me back to Grandma's house. Neither one of us spoke the entire way there.

When we got back, the first thing Grandma wanted to know was why my hair was not done. The only thing Angela told her was that I did not want to get it done. As soon as she left, I told Grandma the whole story. She stayed up late that night, pressing my hair so that it would look nice for Easter Sunday.

I WAS GETTING READY to graduate from the eighth grade. I had applied and been accepted to the second hardest high school in the city. It was different from the neighborhood high schools. It was a college preparatory high school. You had to have good grades and be accepted to go there. It was a one hour bus ride away on the public bus system, but I did not care. This was the best thing I had done in my life and I had done it all by myself. I had filled out and mailed the application without help. I was so excited when I got my acceptance letter in the mail.

Everybody that I told was really happy for me because they all knew that not just anybody went there. I had one cousin who was especially excited for me. You would have thought I had been accepted to medical or law school the way he acted. He said he was telling everybody he knew that his cousin had been accepted to the school.

Eighth grade graduation day had finally arrived. I had already called Angela and told her about it and she said she would be there. Grandma could not go because my uncle was graduating from high school on the same day, at almost the same time. I rode to the graduation with my neighbor, whose daughter was also graduating.

What started as a happy day ended as a sad day. Angela did not show for the graduation. I kept looking for her in the crowd of people but did not see her. I was sure I would see her after it was over. Maybe it was just too crowded for me to see her, but I knew she would see me when they called my name.

I could not believe it; she had lied to me again. She always said she was going to do something, and then she would not do it. How could she miss my graduation? I wanted her to see I was not bad anymore and show her my diploma. Now she could be proud of me. All the other kids had somebody there for them, except me. I was so embarrassed. Once again, I had to pretend that something important to me did not matter. How come she did not love me?

With all the excitement of my uncle graduating from high school, nobody even asked to see my diploma. I wished Angela would have just told me she was not coming. I would not have even bothered going. I would have saved myself the embarrassment.

WHEN I WAS THIRTEEN, a man showed up on Grandma's porch, claiming to be my father. I could not believe it--I had a father! I heard him and Grandma talking in the living room. He said he wanted to see his daughter. He told Grandma how he had contacted her old neighbors to find out where she had moved. Grandma called me into the living room. I pretended I had not overheard them talking.

He did not look anything like I thought he would. I imagined my father to be a really tall man, and skinny like me, but this man was pretty much the opposite. He was the same height as me and he had a big stomach. He had a big, black bushy moustache and a giant smile with pretty teeth.

When I came into the room, he stood up, looked at me and said he was my father. He then hugged me really tight. It was like a dream coming true. I could not wait until I saw my brothers again. Now I had a daddy just like them.

My father used to be a police officer, but now he

ran his own business. He came back the next week and picked me up. He took me to his business to meet his wife and his other children. This was not his first wife, and he had many children. One of them was the same age as me.

My father came back for several weekends and picked me up. He took me to his house. He lived downtown in a high rise apartment that overlooked the river. It was the most beautiful sight I had ever seen. I had never known anybody that lived like that. At night, the lights gleamed across the water and here I was this high up, looking at them sparkle.

I never got to stay overnight with him, but he kept coming back to get me, weekend after weekend. He even let me help in his shop sometimes. I felt so important. I was somebody. I had a father who was important, so that made me important.

One weekend, after almost two months, Grandma told me that my father would not be coming anymore to pick me up. I cried. I had been as good as I knew how to be so that he would love me and always want me. I did not know what I had done wrong. What was wrong with me? Angela did not want me, and now my father did not want me. Was I that ugly? Was I that bad? If only I was prettier, I knew they would both want me. I did not even get a chance to call him Daddy. I hated being me.

I had just watched a movie about a little boy who was the son of the devil. He had a marking on his head of 666. He was really bad in the movie. I thought maybe I was really the devil's child and my father realized it. I searched my head for the 666 mark. I never found it.

I WAS SIXTEEN NOW. It felt a little strange because other girls I knew that were my age had or were going to have a sweet sixteen party, but nobody had said anything about a celebration for me on what is supposed to be an exciting birthday. Angela did not even call to wish me a happy birthday. I guess she forgot again. I tried to tell myself it did not matter, but deep down, it really did.

I think Grandma and her sisters were waiting for me to turn out like Angela. On so many occasions they said it. I would hear them say how I was just like her. I did not like Angela and I certainly did not want to be like her. To them, since I was sixteen, that meant I would be getting pregnant soon and wind up on drugs. I would show them. I would never let that happen to me.

I had a boyfriend now but he was much older than me. I met him on the bus one day while I was riding home from school. I could not believe he liked me because boys never noticed me in that kind of way. I was tall and still very skinny.

All my clothes were hand–me-downs from some agency that gave Grandma free clothes for me. The pants were almost always too short and too big in the waist and hips. How come I could not have been shorter and have a nice body? Maybe the clothes would have fit better and not look like they belonged to someone else.

I already knew that I was not pretty because the kids at school called me ugly all the time and no one in my family thought I was pretty. They never said it directly to me, but they never said I was pretty, so they must have thought I was ugly. I had heard them tell my little sisters how cute they were, but not me. I had some cousins in another state and I knew the family thought they were pretty enough to be models. I did not like what I saw in the mirror. I was the ugly duckling in the family. My boyfriend made me feel pretty. He said that I was the prettiest girl he knew. I knew he was not telling the truth, but it made me feel good to hear it.

The first time I saw him I was on the bus on my way home from school and he asked for my phone number. I told him to give me his instead. I was not sure if I could have boys calling the house because Grandma never told me whether or not I could. I was not even sure if I could have a boyfriend, so I kept him a secret. After about a week of talking on the phone and sometimes seeing each other on the bus, he asked me to be his girlfriend. I accepted. I began lying to Grandma about where I went after school so I could have some time to spend with him.

It was not long before he started telling me he loved me. I told him I loved him, too. I did not know if I really loved him. What did love feel like? Nobody had ever told me that they loved me before. I liked seeing him and spending time with him, so maybe I was in love. Beats me, but I liked the way it sounded and how it made me feel when he said it. I felt beautiful when he said it. I felt special. He bought me flowers and my favorite candy. Sometimes he caught the bus to my school, just so he could ride on the bus with me after school. He definitely loved me to do all that. He told me he knew that he was going to marry me when I graduated from high school. He was four years older than me and had already graduated from high school. I would not graduate until I was eighteen.

I was still a virgin but my boyfriend said that if I loved him then I should show him. He said that when people love each other they did special things for one another. I knew he was talking about sex. At school, I heard the girls in the bathroom talking about sex. The only thing I knew about sex was what I had heard and what I had read about. No one had talked to me about it, but I knew some people that were having sex. I had not been told to save myself for marriage. I did not want to lose my boyfriend. I finally had someone in my life that truly loved me, and I was not going to lose him.

After a few months of having sex, I missed my period. I must have miscalculated this month. I told my boyfriend that I thought I was pregnant. He said he was careful every time, so I could not be pregnant. I waited and sure enough, I did not get my period again. What was I going to do? I could not have a baby. Everybody already thought I was going to be like Angela when I grew up. So this was more proof for them that I would be like her if I had a baby as a teenager. She was sixteen when she had me and now here I was sixteen and pregnant. I was never going to be like her!

When I knew without question that I was pregnant, I told my boyfriend again. He asked me what I was going to do. I already knew. I wanted an abortion. I did not tell anybody else what was going on. He gave me the money and I made the appointment. The day of the appointment, he could not go with me. He had been put in jail for a crime he had committed prior to our meeting. I was scared to get the abortion, but I was more scared to have a baby. When I got to the clinic, they asked who was picking me up. I lied and told them that my mom was.

The procedure was horrible. They had this thing that sounded like a vacuum and felt like one, too. I was sure they were going to pull all of my insides out. It hurt like crazy. A nurse held my hand since I was alone. I looked up at the ceiling and cried silently the entire time. The tears rolled down the side of my face into my ears. This was not supposed to happen to me. I only wanted to do the opposite of what Angela had done. I guess Grandma and her sisters were right about me, but they would never know it. I might have gotten pregnant young but they would never know and I surely was not going to wind up on drugs.

After the procedure was over, I was taken to a recovery room where I had to stay for an hour. There were lots of women in there, some young like me and some older. I sat alone. I did not want to talk to them. My stomach was cramping from the procedure. The nurse said I needed to rest and not to do any strenuous activities for the next few days. I did not have a ride home, but when they released me, I pretended my ride was outside. I walked almost fifteen blocks to get home. I was hoping I did not bleed to death on the way. The pain was almost unbearable. I had walked farther than this many times, but today it seemed like I was walking fifteen miles instead of fifteen blocks.

When I got home, I had to pretend like it was a normal day for me even though I was in pain and should be resting. Grandma did not believe in kids lying around in the middle of the day, so I could not just get in the bed. I told her I had cramps really bad. That was the only way I knew she would not say anything about me getting in bed. I would be glad when the pain was over. I did not want to do anything except take some pain medication and go to sleep.

It was my senior year of high school. I had made it. I did not always have the best grades, but other than the school, no one knew it since I never had to show my report card to anyone. Grandma would just ask what grades I got and I would always tell her all A's and B's. My senior year seemed a lot easier, so I really did get all A's and B's. I did not know what I would do after high school was over. A lot of people I knew worked in the automotive plants, so I would probably be able to get a good job there. My cousin Vickie worked in the office of one of the plants. I typed pretty well, so maybe I could work in the office instead of on the assembly line.

You would think since I went to a college preparatory school that college would have been on my mind. It was not. My highest goal in life was to graduate from high school and not be like Angela. One day someone asked me where I was going to school. I did not have an answer since I had not considered it. At that moment, a thought occurred to me. Angela did not go to college, so this would definitely make me different than her. I would go to college.

I did not know how I was going to pay for it. Since I did not do as well as I could have in school, I did not think I could get a scholarship. For the first time, I wished I would have had someone pushing me to do my best. No one had held me accountable for getting the best grades I could make. Sometimes I was close to flunking out and nobody even knew it. Whenever I got that close, I would work hard so that I would not have to change schools. With my school being a college preparatory technical school, a certain grade point average had to be maintained. I had always filled out my own paperwork and signed it also. So as long as the school never called the house, I was good to go.

Going to college would definitely ensure that I would not wind up like Angela, and I could have a career. The thought of college had changed my entire way of thinking. I thought of all the things I could become. A pharmacist, a lawyer, an accountant--I did not know what, but I could become somebody. The possibilities were endless. Maybe I could even be famous! I was definitely going to college. Someway, somehow, I was going to make this happen. I was meeting with my high school counselor to find out what I needed to do. I applied to a few schools that I qualified for. Now I just had to figure out how to pay tuition.

I was accepted into two of the colleges I applied to. I decided to tell Angela that I was going to college. I did not know why I even bothered. She started asking me how I was going to pay for it. I told her I did not know. She said I should just go to a community college and then try to go to a university later, because nobody had that kind of money. I told her that I was not asking her for the money. I already knew she did not have it, but I did not say that to her. I told her I just wanted her to know that I was going.

She started telling me how I thought I was better than her. She wanted to know if I thought I was too good for community college. She made me so sick. Man, I hated her! I did not even know why I said anything to her at all. I was sure she could care less if I went to college or not. She had never supported me in the past, why would she be different now? She just did not get it; all I wanted her to do was say that she was proud of me. I did not want money from her. If she could not love me, at least she could be proud of me. I guess that was too much to ask. I would show her. I was going to that school even if I had to work all day and all night to pay for it. I would not be like her and just accept whatever came my way. I was going to make my own way. Who was she to tell me what I could not do?

I filed for and received financial aid. It was really happening for me; I was going to college! This ugly, poor daughter of a heroin addict was going to college. Financial aid would cover everything except my books, room and board. I took out a student loan to cover the dorm room and my books. I was awarded work study so I thought that should be good enough to cover food expenses.

High school graduation came and went without Angela in attendance. No surprise there. I would never be like her when I was a mother. My children would know that I loved them and I would tell them how proud I was of them when they did something good.

THAT SUMMER, BEFORE I was to begin college, I went to Angela's house to look after my brothers and sisters. Angela said she had to go to the hospital for a few weeks and did not have anyone to watch them for that long. I did not get to spend much time with them, so I was more than happy to go. Angela left me in charge of them, her house and her car. I thought this was her way of trying to make up for missing my graduation.

My brothers, sisters and I were having so much fun together. I felt like the momma again, like I did before I went to live with Grandma. Even though they were all older now, they looked up to me. I was happy and sad all at the same time. I was happy because we were together and sad because I thought about how Angela never came back to get me so we could all live together. She kept them; why did she not keep me? Oh well, it was too late for that now anyway. Plus, I would be at college in a couple of months.

It was really good for the first two weeks. One

day it was raining really hard and my youngest brother called from school asking if I could pick them up. I said sure. My twin brothers and I got into the car and headed to the school. On our way there, we were laughing and the windows had fogged up. Out of nowhere, a car ran right into us. We got hit on the passenger side towards the back of the car. The car was a small two-door hatchback so it was not very big. I was shaken and stunned. I had never been in a car accident before.

My brothers and I got out of the car and so did the lady from the other car. She started apologizing to us. I looked at Angela's car, and it was in really bad shape. We were supposed to exchange information, but the lady said she did not have her license and insurance information with her. This was okay with me because Angela did not leave me any insurance information, so I did not have any, either. I gave her my phone number and then I wrote down her name and license plate number to give to Angela. The rear bumper from our car was laying on the ground. I told my brother to pick it up and put it in the trunk.

So much time had passed since the accident and the phone call to pick the kids up at school that my brother and sisters had walked home from school. It was not raining anymore; the sun was shining. When we got back to the house, they came outside to find out why we never showed up and they saw the car was all messed up. They could not believe it. That night, I called Angela to tell her what happened. She was very angry and was yelling. I knew she would be. I tried to explain what happened but she did not want to hear it. She told me to come to the hospital tomorrow and pick her up. Since I did not drop her off, she had to tell me the name and location of the hospital. It was not a hospital, it was a rehab center. She was trying to get off drugs.

When I got there to pick her up, she was shocked at the condition of the car. It was drivable, but looked really bad. I got out of the driver's seat and she got in it. One of my brothers was in the back seat. She asked me why I did not stop. I told her I tried but something was wrong with the brakes. She said there is nothing wrong with the brakes and stepped on them really hard. The car was not stopping that fast and we were sliding on the road. I told her they were not working that good. My brother was touching my arm and trying to make me laugh. I kept my composure, even though it was funny seeing the look on her face when she tried to stop. She turned and looked at me. I just hunched my shoulders and said I told you.

Angela stayed home for two days and then went back to rehab. After she left, my brother told me that Angela said the only reason I came to watch them was so I could drive her car, and now I have wrecked it. I could not believe she told him that. She did not realize how I always dreamed about living with them and how often I wondered why she did not come to get me. I did not have a good life when I lived with Angela, but she had my brothers and sisters, so it seemed to me that I was supposed to be there also. I told my brother that was a lie and I was here because I wanted to be.

One day I went outside and there was a note on the front door. I read it and it was an eviction notice. It said that we had three days to vacate the premises or all our things would be put out. I did not know what to do. I called Grandma and told her about the eviction notice. She told me to call Angela so that she could come home and handle the matter. She told me there was nothing I could do about the eviction at this point since it was a court order. I tried calling Angela but did not get her. I left a message. She did not call back. I called her again later; she did not take my call.

The next day, I called again. I was nervous because she was not calling me back. I did not know what to do with my brothers and sisters.

I was leaving for college in two weeks, so I had somewhere to go, but what about them? I called Grandma again and told her I could not get in touch with Angela. She told me what to do. She said she could not take my brothers and sisters because she had gotten too old to take care of young kids anymore. She told me the only thing I could do was call Child Protective Services and they would come and get my brothers and sisters. How could Angela not tell me that she was behind on her payments?

I sat my brothers and sisters down and tried to explain to them the best I could that I had to call someone to pick them up because we could no longer live here. They asked if I was coming with them. I told them no and that it was time for me to go to college. We were all crying. This was too much for me. How was I supposed to make the call for them to go to foster care? This was not right, but I had no choice.

The next morning, I called the number Grandma had given me. After a few hours, a white car pulled up and a lady came in. She had me sign some papers and give her as much information about Angela as I could. After I was done, she was ready to take my brothers and sisters. They had packed a few of their things. I hugged each one of them and we tried not to cry. I watched them get in the white car and I could not stop the tears from running down my face. They were all looking at me. How would they ever forgive me for this? I was sending them to some unknown place. They waved to me and I waved back. The car pulled off. I could see them looking back at me. I tried to smile while I was waving, but I did not feel happy. I had no idea where they were going to sleep tonight. I called Angela and left her another message about what had just happened. How come she had not called me back? I left and went back to Grandma's house to wait for school to start. It was a long two weeks.

MY FIRST WEEK ON the campus was unbelievable. It still had not sunk in all the way that this was my school. I was a college coed. I had a dorm room and a roommate. This was so different from high school. The dorm room was just that, a room. There were two twin beds, a double closet and a long desk made for two. I felt like I had my own studio apartment, except that the bathroom was not in my room but down the hall. I did not care; at least I was here. Being on campus was like its own little world--pretty much everything I needed was right here.

My first year of college passed without incident. At the end of the year, I went back to Grandma's house. It was a hard and long summer. After living on campus and having the independence that comes with it, it was hard to conform to the rules. I did not have a curfew on campus and we would hang out as late as we wanted. Here, I was subject to curfew again, and chores.

One evening, I was all set to go to a party with

some of my friends. We had planned to arrive really late and then go to the after-party. They were going to pick me up around eleven thirty. I got myself ready and was waiting for them.

Grandma had seen me getting ready. When it was almost eleven and I had not gone anywhere, she asked me why I was still home if I was going to a party. I told her I would get picked up at eleven thirty. She looked at me and said I would not be getting picked up that late from her house. She said if I had not gone by eleven, then I would be staying home.

After experiencing the freedom of college, I felt a little cocky. I told her I would be going to the party when my friends came. I felt that I was grown at that point and she could not tell me what to do. I had never heard Grandma yell and she did not yell then. She simply said to me that if I left after eleven, not to come back and then she walked away and went into her room. I was pretty sure this was a not an empty threat. I was angry, but I was not fool enough to test her because I did not have anywhere else to live, so I called my friends and told them not to come. I went to my room and sat there angry and defeated. I knew right then that I would not be coming back there for my next summer break.

During that summer, I found out where all my brothers and sisters were. The twins were within walking distance of Grandma's house. My other brother and two sisters were together but lived too far to walk and I did not have a car. I was happy to know they were okay. I had not talked to Angela in quite some time. With the twins nearby, I got a chance to visit often, and I also got a few chances to visit with my other brother and two sisters.

My second year of college was a lot different. I joined with a group of young ladies on campus as a mock sorority. We were associated with one of the fraternities on campus as their sisterhood club. We did many things together--partying, drinking and just hanging out. I began smoking marijuana. I was getting drunk and high only on weekends at first. Weekend partying turned into weekday partying. There was a girl on campus who actually sold marijuana. She befriended me and my closest friend at the time. We were high almost every day.

I was beginning to get noticed by the guys on campus and I liked it. It made me feel beautiful and desired. There was nothing wrong with that. The problem came when they stopped noticing and began approaching me. I took their advances as more than a simple liking. I still had a desire for someone to love me, so I allowed many of them to have sex with me, because I still had the mentality of sex being love. In my mind, if they had sex with me, that meant they had deeper feelings. It also made me popular on campus. I did not stop to think about what kind of popularity I was gaining. It did not even cross my mind that not all popularity was good popularity. Because my self esteem was low, I was easy prey for those who intended to just use me. I was getting a reputation and did not even know it. Instead, I felt special when those guys wanted to be with me. For me, it became a way to believe that I was beautiful and loved. The guys hung around for a while but they never developed a deep relationship with me. I was still looking for love in all the wrong places.

One day as I was walking to class, I realized that I was slowly becoming Angela. Even though I was in college, I was on my way to becoming a drug addict. The very thing I was trying not to become, I was becoming. How did this happen without me realizing it? Deep inside, I knew the answer to my question. I had allowed myself to believe that because it was only marijuana that it was not the same as heroin. Addiction is addiction, and I was definitely headed towards addiction if I did not stop. I already had a cousin that I got high with sometimes that had become an addict. Someone laced her marijuana with crack cocaine and she did not know it. Now she was going to rehab. If I did not stop, I might be next. I had to get myself together. I would not smoke anymore.

I found out that it was easier to say I would not use drugs anymore than to actually do it. I had not smoked any in a while, but at parties when it was offered to me, I took it because I did not want to seem lame in front of my friends. I smoked with them and got high again. What was wrong with me? Why was I doing what I did not want to do just so I could keep calling these people my friends? If they were my real friends, then it would not matter to them if I smoked or not. I was just kidding myself. These parties that I had been attending were for those that wanted to get high and have fun while high. I stopped going to the parties and lost most of those so-called friends. I was going to concentrate on my schoolwork. All that partying and getting high had caused me to be on academic probation.

I HAD GOTTEN MYSELF back on track and off academic probation. I had even bought myself an old used car. I spent most of my time alone. It was hard to make new friends when you had a reputation like mine. I had not been involved with any guys for quite some time. One day, as I was walking through the Student Union, I saw this handsome guy that I had never seen before sitting on one of the couches. He smiled at me, and I smiled back. I kept walking. He got up and came over and started walking next to me. I did not say a word. He asked my name and told me his was Carl. He was mild-mannered and charming. I liked him already. He walked me across campus and then asked for my number. I gave it to him.

Carl and I had been dating for a month now. He told me I was everything he had been looking for and that he loved me and wanted to marry me. I told him that I loved him, too. No one had said anything about marrying me since my first boyfriend. I spent every day with Carl. He was my whole world. I saw people looking at us when we were together. I did not care because I was not who I used to be. I was happy and in love.

One afternoon, I was supposed to be at work, but had decided not to go. I was headed to the library and cut through the Student Union. I saw Carl sitting down, and there was some girl all over him. I watched him kiss and hug her. My heart dropped. I stood still for a moment, trying to decide what to do. Before I knew it, I was walking over to them. I said hello to him and he said hi and that he would catch up with me later. Catch up with me later? If some guy had tried to do me like that in the past, I would have told him off, but I could not find the words to do that now. I just walked away.

I did not hear from Carl until the next day. He started apologizing and telling me how sorry he was and that he never wanted to hurt me. Deep inside, I knew he was lying to me, but I loved him and did not want to lose him. He always knew the right words to say to me.

He had done it again! I caught Carl with another woman. Why did I keep taking myself through this drama? I was breaking up with him this time. I called and told him and he said okay. I was devastated. He did not even try to convince me to stay with him. I hated my life. What was the point of living? I was so unhappy all the time. I wanted to totally change who I was.

There was a group of girls on campus who went to Bible Study and seemed nice. People liked them and respected them. I wanted to be like them – respected. I approached two of them one day and asked if I could hang with them and go to Bible Study. They looked at me like I was crazy. One of them proceeded to tell me that they would not want to be seen hanging out with someone like me. My reputation had preceded me. Even though I no longer slept around, people still remembered.

I felt so embarrassed and ashamed of myself. For me those girls represented God, so the silent message they sent to me was loud and clear. I was so horrible that not even God wanted to say He knew me. Carl did not love me anymore. Angela and my father did not love me, and now God? I saw no reason to keep living my worthless life. I went to the store and bought three bottles of sleeping pills. I parked my car on the far back side of campus, where nobody ever went. I started taking the pills. After I took them all, I could feel myself getting sleepy really fast. It was a really hot day, but I kept my windows rolled up. I thought that would make it go faster. I did not know when someone would find my body, but by the time they did, I would be dead. I leaned my seat back some and went to sleep.

A man was opening the door of my car. I did not know who he was. He pulled me out the car and said the ambulance was coming. How did he know what I had done or that I needed an ambulance? The next thing I knew, I was being loaded onto an ambulance and rushed to the hospital. I was so sleepy, but the EMTs forced me to stay awake. In the emergency room, the doctors pumped my stomach. They asked me for emergency contact information. I did not know why, but I gave them Carl's phone number. My suicide attempt was a failure and I could not let Grandma know I had done this.

No one could tell me who the guy was that found me. Apparently, he left after the ambulance showed up. Thanks to him, my whole plan was ruined. Surprisingly, Carl showed up and had his brother with him. He told me that he loved me and did not want me to die.

It had been six months since I tried to kill myself. Carl has just given me an engagement ring. He had met my family, but he did not get along with them. I did not care. He loved me and we were going to get married. He still cheated on me, but I knew once we got married it would be different. Carl said we had to go to City Hall to get married because we did not have money for a wedding. That was not what I had in mind, but at least we would be married.

After a year and a half of off-and-on-again dating, the day had arrived for us to get married. We had not told anyone that we were eloping. Carl thought we should wait until after we were married to announce it, so I agreed. At City Hall there were lots of other couples waiting to get married. They took us all into a large room and had everyone stand side by side. We all repeated the vows at one time. All of a sudden, I changed my mind. I did not want to marry Carl. I thought it was too late so I kept saying the vows. With every word, I knew this was all wrong. We were done with the vows and now we just had to sign the papers. We signed them and headed back to the school campus. I did not feel married. There was no excitement or anyone to celebrate with us.

Later that evening, Carl got a call and said he would be back in a little while. He did not have a car and had not asked to borrow mine. When he left, I followed him. He headed to the front of the campus. He did not see me. He was getting picked up, and I recognized the car. It was one of the girls he had cheated on me with. This was unbelievable. We just got married today and he was spending the evening with her. Why did I think marriage would change him because nothing had changed. Nothing at all.

Three months after we were married, I was pregnant. I did not want to tell Carl, but then I thought maybe this would help. It did not. As a matter of fact, it seemed as though he was the least attracted to me that he had ever been. He was gone almost every night. When he was around he made me feel horrible about myself. What happened to the charming guy that I met in the Student Union?

With the baby coming, Carl and I needed to find another place to live. We found a house to rent. Ironically, it was only about a mile from the projects that I used to live in. It was off the same main street, so I passed the projects almost every day. Since we had more room, I wanted to try to get my sisters. They were both in high school now. They could share a bedroom. We did not have enough room to get my younger brother. The twins were out of foster care now. We applied as foster parents and were approved. By being family, the process went a little faster. Within two months, they moved in.

I finally had the baby, and it was a little boy. He was the most beautiful baby I had ever seen, and he was mine. Carl came for the delivery and brought flowers to the hospital the day after I delivered the baby. He was finally being the Carl I first met, charming and nice.

It did not last long. He seemed angrier than ever. He told me I was too focused on the baby. He had started hitting me. I was too embarrassed to tell anyone. I did not know what I could do that would make him happy. It seemed like he got mad if I talked to anyone. He said I was trying to show him up and make them not like him. That was not the case at all, I was only being myself. I had started to not talk or smile when others were around. It was easier to act like that, and then I did not have to worry about him being angry with me.

Over time, I saw this did not matter; nothing I did made him happy. I was sad all the time but tried to pretend to others that I was happy. Sometimes, he did not come home for a few days. I knew where he was because the woman he was with called me sometimes just to tell me he was with her. This same woman had slashed the tires on my car before and we almost had a physical fight over him. I felt like such a fool, but I did not want to admit I had made a mistake in marrying him.

Things were getting worse and worse between me and Carl. We argued all the time. On one particular day, we were arguing because he wanted to take my car and go somewhere. I would not give him the keys. He said he wanted to go over his mother's house. I told him I would drop him off but that he was not taking the car. I left the baby with my sisters and left to drop him off. We were still arguing.

A few blocks down the road he hit me while I was driving. He hit me so hard in my eye that it felt like it had fallen out of the socket. I swerved across the opposite lanes of traffic. Fortunately, there was no oncoming traffic. I managed to pull off the road. I yelled at him, and he told me he was going to drive. When he got out of the car to come over to the driver's side, I pulled off. As I drove off, I realized I had nowhere to go except back to the house.

He must have run back because I was only in the house a few minutes before he came storming in. He was yelling and cursing like a madman. He knocked me down to the floor and stood over me, yelling at the top of his lungs. I was jammed up against the wall, so there was nowhere for me to move. I rolled myself into a ball because I did not know if he was going to kick me. My sisters were standing there, watching and screaming for him to stop. One of them was holding the baby. Maybe because they were standing there, Carl did not kick me. He grabbed the car keys and left. I took the baby from my sister and went to the bathroom to check out my eye. It was not out of the socket, nor was it bleeding. It was swollen and sore but it would be okay. I told my sisters that everything would be all right; we were just having a bad fight. I could tell they did not believe me.

Carl had bought two guns. One was a handgun and the other was a shotgun. He said he bought them for protection since we did not live in the best of neighborhoods. One night when he came home from work, I was in the bed with the baby lying next to me. He came into the bedroom but did not turn on the light. I heard him walk over to the window. He had not said anything to me directly, but he said aloud that he hated me. The next thing I heard was him cocking the shotgun. I grabbed the baby and held him tightly. I thought he was going to shoot me. I lay very still, holding my breath. I was sure only a few minutes had passed, but it felt like an hour. All of a sudden, he just left the room. I did not get out of the bed until morning. Carl never came back in the room that night, but I did not hear the shotgun go off. He was not there when I got up. I felt like I was living in some crazy nightmare.

Two years had passed since Carl and I got married. I had finally finished all my college coursework and would graduate. It had not been an easy process. I had managed to reach this milestone in spite of dealing with all the issues in my marriage, having a baby and working full-time.

Graduation day had come and I was excited. It seemed like a lifetime ago that I decided to go to college. Carl was being very nice to me today. He had bought me flowers and was taking all of us to dinner later. Maybe the stress of me being in school had been difficult for him. When we got to the graduation, I took my seat and could see my family. There was Carl and the baby, and my brothers and sisters were there. I was hoping that Angela might show up. I even took a chance and went by my father's shop and gave him an invitation. There was still a part of me hoping that he would accept me again. Now he had a reason to be proud of me because I would be a college graduate. They were both no-shows. I had to stop setting myself up for a letdown.

Carl was nice to me for the entire week after

graduation, and then he started being mean and nasty again. A few months after graduation, I finally decided I was leaving Carl. I asked Grandma if the baby and I could stay with her for awhile. She said yes. My younger sister had moved out and my other sister, Jocelyn, had two daughters by now. I told her my plans, so she made provisions to move with her boyfriend. This was very hard for me because she was my best friend. Now that she was older, we talked about everything. I had cared for her two children as if they were my own. When I got my son ready for daycare, I got hers ready for daycare, if she could not. When I fed him, I fed them. When I shopped for him, I shopped for them. All three children were one year apart, so they were very close, just like brother and sisters.

I was not telling Carl that I was moving. I knew if I told him, he would not let me leave easily, if at all. Every day while he was at work, I was packing my things and storing them in the basement under the stairs. I knew he would not see the bags there.

I had planned my departure very carefully, and the day had finally arrived. I had rented a moving truck and taken the day off work. I got up that morning as usual and prepared the kids for daycare. I dropped them off and waited for Carl to leave for work. I drove past the house to make sure he was gone. I went to the truck rental place and picked up the truck. I called the people who were helping me move and they met me at the house. We got all my bags from out of the basement and the few things I did not pack. We loaded up all the furniture from all the rooms except for the bedroom. I did not want to take that furniture. I did not want to remember anything about the bedroom or sleep in the bed anymore. I told Jocelyn she could take the furniture from her bedroom.

IT DID NOT TAKE Carl long to figure out where I had gone. Grandma had already told me how it would play out when he found me. She said he would call several times. The first few calls he would be nice, but if I did not come to the phone he would start to get angry. She also told me he would use our son to try to put a guilt trip on me. If that did not work, she said he would show up at her house. She wanted to know from me, before all the drama began, what I was trying to accomplish. I told her plain and simple, I did not want to be with him anymore. I had not told her that he hit me, but I had a feeling she already knew.

Just as Grandma predicted, Carl did all the things she said. When he came to the house, it was dark outside. He was out there, ranting and raving like a madman. Grandma told him if he did not leave she would call the police. It was a wonder the neighbors had not already called the police. Her threat made him leave.

I stayed at Grandma's house for six months.

It took me that long to save up enough money to move into an apartment. I had to pay first and last month's rent, plus the current rent in order to move in. It was a two bedroom apartment, just big enough for me and my son.

It was getting tough to pay all my bills, the rent and take care of my son. Carl would not help me raise our son. He said if I wanted to be a single mom, then I needed to handle my business as a single mom. It was not right, but it was not like I could call and tell my creditors or landlord that. They wanted their money, regardless of what was going on in my personal life. Having a college degree was not doing me much good because I was underpaid. I knew people who did not have a degree that were getting paid more than me.

I had stopped paying my car insurance and had cut everything to bare bones. It was not enough. If I did not do something soon, I would get evicted or lose my car. I just had to choose which one I was not going to pay. I could not live in the car with my child, so it looked like the rent won. Of course, if I lost my car, then I would not be able to get to work. There was also the cost of daycare. I was stuck between a rock and a hard place. I knew what I was going to have to do to get some extra money, but I did not want to do it.

I called and made an appointment at the welfare office. I could not believe it had come to this, but I was in no position to let my pride get in the way. I had a child to take care of. On the day of my appointment, I gathered all my information and went to the office. It seemed like there were a thousand people, mostly women and children, in the lobby. Even though I had an appointment, I still had to take a number. What was the point of having an appointment? If I had known that, I would have shown up earlier. After waiting more than two hours, they finally called my name.

Once I was in the back, I sat at the desk of the lady who called my name. She was short and heavy-set with an old-looking wig. She was not that old, but her clothes and wig made her look older. She did not look at me much while she asked me questions. It seemed like she wanted my entire life history. I gave her all my paperwork and signed where she told me to on the forms she had given me. When I was done, she told me I should know soon if I had been approved or not. In the meantime, she gave me some emergency food stamps.

As I left the office, all I could think about was Angela. It seemed like the harder I tried not to be like her, the more I became like her. That day, it felt like I should have just given into what seemed to be inevitable, but then I looked down at my son smiling at me, and I decided not to. He had no clue how hard it was to take care of him by myself and the thoughts of escape that sometimes went through my mind. But when I saw his big round eyes, his beautiful smile and heard his adorable laugh, all those thoughts left my mind.

I had been approved for welfare. They would give me a monthly check and food stamps. The check by itself was not enough to cover all my expenses, but combined with my paycheck, I would be able to pay my main bills. I was so relieved, but ashamed. Here I was, a college graduate, receiving a welfare check. I was not telling anyone that I was on welfare.

I RAN INTO CARL on occasion at Jocelyn's house because she was engaged to his brother. They were opposites of each other. He was always smiling and laughing and was nice to my sister- -not just in front of other people, either. She and I were best friends and we talked several times a day. One day while at Jocelyn's house, Carl and I got into an argument about my son. Right in the middle of the argument, he slapped me. I yelled at him and told him he could not treat me like that anymore. I called the police. He actually had the nerve to stay right there and say they were not going to believe me, anyway. His brother was standing right there when it happened, so I asked him if he would be my witness that Carl had hit me. He said he did not want to get involved. I went outside and waited in my car for the police.

When the police arrived, I got out of my car and went over to theirs. Carl came outside. I told them I was the one that called and that I wanted to press charges. Carl immediately started denying that he hit me and said he was only trying to visit his son. While I was trying to tell the police Carl was lying, one of them asked me where he had hit me. I pointed to the side of my face that he had hit. I did not realize it, but my lip was bleeding and the side of my face was still red. They arrested Carl and put him in the police car. He started yelling that he could not believe I would do this in front of his son. I stood there looking at him like he was a fool. Now he was concerned about what his son saw? He was not thinking about that when he slapped me.

Since I was pressing charges against Carl, I thought I would have to go to court, but fortunately I did not. He agreed to take domestic violence courses. For that, he would not get any jail time or anything on his record, if he completed the courses. I was glad because I did not want him to go to jail. I just wanted him to know that he could not push me around or hit me anymore.

It has been almost two years since I left Carl and a year since I called the police on him. I still saw him often at Jocelyn's house. He had not tried to hit me anymore. I noticed that he was nicer to me and took more interest in our son. He even gave me money for him on occasion. He kept hinting that he would like to get back together and that he still loved me. As badly as he treated me when we were together, I should not have even considered us being together again, but I did. We were only separated. We never got divorced. I toyed with the idea. Maybe we could try to make it work and be a happy family.

The next time I went over to Jocelyn's house, I told him my decision. I would like to try our marriage again. I told him he had to agree never to hit me again, and he said he would not. We hugged and kissed. It felt just like the first time we kissed. I was so happy, I could not stop smiling. We announced to my sister and his brother that we were getting back together. His brother was happy and gave us both a hug. Jocelyn hugged us but I was not sure if she was really happy or not. If she was not, I knew it was because of everything that had happened in the past. Later, I asked her in private and she told me she was happy for me.

Carl moved in with me and my son the very next week. I called the welfare office and told them I did not need assistance anymore. I was not telling Carl I was on welfare. I did not even tell Jocelyn, so I was certainly not telling him. I tried to make everything as comfortable as possible for Carl. I wanted our marriage to work, and my son was so happy his daddy was living with us again. This felt good and right. Carl had even bought me another wedding ring.

It did not take long for us to start arguing. Somehow we managed to find something to argue about every day. I dreaded going home after work. Before we split up, I used to get mad when Carl did not come home. Now that we were back together, I found myself hoping he did not come home.

Why did we get back together? I had idealized in my mind that he had missed me so much, that everything would be wonderful once we got back together. How wrong I was. I was glad he had not tried to hit me, but I could not take much more of this arguing.

A CO-WORKER OF MINE told me about a job opportunity in Texas. Wow, Texas. I had always wanted to live somewhere else besides Brownwood. I did not have any particular place in mind, just some place where the weather was warmer. I had never even visited Texas, but I knew that it was hot there. I was excited, so I decided to apply. After several phone interviews, I was flown to Texas for a face–to-face interview with a panel of people.

The company was located in a suburb outside of Paledo. It was so beautiful in Texas. The streets were very clean and everything seemed brighter there. The people spoke to you, even if they did not know you. In Brownwood, it was rare for people to speak to someone they did not know. I liked the feel of Texas. If I was hired, the company would put me up in corporate housing for two months and pay my moving expenses. I had never been offered this kind of deal before.

At least if I went to Texas, I would have a good

job and would make more money than I ever made in Brownwood. I could start my life over again. I did not know anybody there except the people who interviewed me for my job. I had already talked to Carl about moving there, and he said he was not going. Secretly inside, I was very happy that he said that. I would truly have a clean start.

It took about a week and a half before I heard back from the company. I got the job! I told Carl I got the job in Texas and that I was going to take it. We both knew what that meant: we were splitting again. With me moving to another state, it would be permanent this time. I was not sure how he felt about it, but I was glad. No more arguing and fighting and it was an opportunity for a better life. I could not wait.

Two weeks before I got ready to leave, Carl told me he had changed his mind and was coming after all. I cannot believe this! Now what? I could not tell him I did not really want him to come. So I went along with the program, hoping that maybe since neither one of us knew anyone there maybe, just maybe, we could give our marriage a fresh start.

I told people I was leaving, and many were happy and optimistic. Others were not so optimistic, so they kindly reminded me that if it did not work out in Texas I could always come back to Brownwood. They must have been crazy. I was not coming back to. I did not care if I had to move somewhere else, I was not coming back, unless it was to visit.

It was almost the end of January on the day we were to leave. Snow and ice was everywhere. I could not wait to go to Texas and leave all of this snow behind. We were driving and had estimated it would take us about three days to get there since we were not driving straight through. There was no need to rush because I would not start work for two weeks. When we got to Texas, the weather was beautiful. We did not need to wear anything heavier than a sweatshirt or a sweater. I love it here.

It had been four months since we moved to Texas and everything had been really good between me and Carl. My job put us in corporate housing until we could get ourselves settled. In the evening, we were home together. We ate dinner together, took walks together. We even talked. We did not talk about our problems, but at least we were talking and not fighting.

Once Carl got a job and started meeting people, our problems began to show up again. He started coming home late and then would lie about where he had been. I had been with him for so long that I knew when he was lying and when he was telling the truth. Next, the secret phone calls started coming, and the unexplained absences.

It was then that I realized my biggest problem had followed me from Brownwood to Paledo but because of my own insecurities, I was too weak to do anything about it. I kept thinking about all the people who thought we would not stay together this time. I thought about those in Brownwood that said I would be back. I could not go back to Brownwood, and I did not want my marriage to fail, in spite of the fact that it was failing.

Carl and I were back to barely talking again. We were more like roommates than husband and wife. Somehow, I had convinced myself that as long as we did not get divorced then I would not be a failure in my marriage. I wanted my son to have what I never have, to be raised by his mother and father, who were together as a family.

JOCELYN WAS COMING TO visit! I was so excited. I could not wait to see my sister, my best friend. My phone bill was always sky high from talking to her every day. Carl's brother is coming also and they were bringing their two daughters. They would stay for just over a week.

I had been sick lately, but I knew it was from the heat. It was only May and it had been over one hundred degrees every day. I was not used to that kind of heat, but I was not going to let that ruin Jocelyn's visit. When they got to Texas, they absolutely loved it. We took them downtown, to restaurants, the movies and swimming at our apartment's pool. We had the best time ever. I was sad when it was time for them to go home. With Jocelyn there, I realized how much I really missed her, but I knew she had to go. After they left, things returned to normal for me and Carl, if you call not talking normal.

When Jocelyn got back to Brownwood, she told me they were thinking about moving to Texas.

This was more exciting to me than when she told me she was coming to visit. She said they would discuss it some more, but she was pretty sure that they were going to do it. She said they hoped to move within the next two months, if they had a place to stay. Our apartment was too small for all of us to live in, so I started looking for an apartment for them to move into. Unlike Brownwood, the deposits for apartments were much cheaper and the apartments were much nicer. I told Jocelyn I would cover the deposit and help them with their moving costs.

I had become pretty good friends with a lady from my job named Sherrie, and I told her how the heat was making me sick. Sherrie said that happened to a lot of people when they could not handle the heat. I decided to go to the doctor. I could not take this heat sickness anymore. The doctor told me I did not have heat sickness; I was pregnant. My mouth almost fell to the floor when she told me I was about six weeks along. Counting back, that took me right to the end of those great four months Carl and I had here in Texas.

I called Jocelyn when I got home and told her the news. She said now it made sense why I had been sick. I did not have morning sickness when I was pregnant with my son, so I did not think that I would have morning sickness if I ever got pregnant again.

When Carl came home, I told him I was pregnant. You have thought I was telling him the neighbor's dog was pregnant. The only thing he asked was when I was due and when did I find out. No excitement, no emotion. Of course, with things the way they were between us, why would I expect anything different?

The time had finally arrived for Jocelyn to move to Texas. I rented them an apartment in the complex we were living in when they came to visit. This way, I knew for sure they would love it. It was great having her here. It was just like old times in Brownwood. I could go visit her and see my nieces. It had been tough moving to a place where I did not know anyone personally.

I called and told Angela that I was pregnant. I asked her if she wanted to come and care for the baby for the first two months. I told her I would pay her. She agreed to come and help. She had babysat my son when he was a baby. She was not the same person she had been when I was a kid. She had been clean from drugs for about nine years now. She had done a good job with my son, so I was sure she would do a good job with this baby. She has never been to Texas before, so this would give her a chance to see what my new home was like.

Jocelyn told Angela about her plans to move to Texas. She said that Angela told her that it would not be a smart move for her. Unlike me, Jocelyn would not be coming here with a job already in place. She also told me that Angela said I was trying to tear the family apart. She said it I was bad enough that I had left, now I was trying to convince Jocelyn to leave.

What was Angela talking about? I had not convinced Jocelyn to move to Texas; that was her own idea and decision. And why would she say I was tearing the family apart? She did not say that when I left, but now that Jocelyn wanted to come she was concerned. Jocelyn told me not to worry about any of that. She knew it was her decision and she was definitely coming.

JOCELYN WAS HERE NOW and all settled in. She had enrolled her oldest daughter in kindergarten. We visited each other often and, of course, talked every day on the phone. It was good to have her here.

The time was getting closer for me to have the baby. Angela told me she was preparing to come and wanted to know when I would book her ticket. She did not know it but I was angry about her comments to Jocelyn concerning me. I told her I did not want her to come. Then I told her I did not like what she said to Jocelyn about me. I reminded her that I had always tried to find a way for me and my brothers and sisters to be in contact with each other. I let her know I did not need her down here causing confusion and problems.

I had enough problems already without her adding to the mix. She did not apologize; she just told me that I was putting Jocelyn in a position that she might not be able to handle. I thought to myself, *what was she talking about?* I told her Jocelyn was doing just fine here in Texas, and it was her decision to move here. I did not convince her to do anything. She was making me mad, so I got off the phone with her.

I did not talk to Angela for a couple of weeks. I was almost within two weeks of my due date. She finally called me and told me she had booked her own ticket and was coming. Now, when I did not want to be bothered with her, she wanted to insist on being a part of my life. I hated to admit it, but I knew where I got my stubbornness and persistence from.

Angela was here now and I had gone into labor. This entire pregnancy had been different than the first one, including the labor. It was a slow process with my son, and he came two weeks past my due date. This time I went into labor about two hours on the evening before my due date. The pain had come fast and hard. I was at home with Angela. Carl was not there. Angela called and told him she was taking me to the hospital. After much pain and four hours later, my baby girl made her grand entrance. She was so beautiful and had a head full of hair. Right before she was born, Carl made it to the hospital.

Angela had been here for three months and was now leaving to go back to Brownwood. When she got back to Brownwood, she called and said that she loved Texas so much that she wanted to move here. She was back one month later with all her things. She moved in with me and Carl. We paid her to take care of the baby. I did not want her to think we were trying to use her. I was glad that I did not have to take my sweet little baby girl to a daycare center so young.

ABOUT FOUR MONTHS AFTER I had my baby, I came home from work one day and I was so exhausted I laid down right in the middle of the living room. I was too tired to even check on my children. It just hit me all of a sudden. I did not feel this way at work. Thankfully, Angela was there, because I did not feel like doing anything for them. After I had been lying on the floor for a couple of hours, Angela asked me if I was okay. I had told her I was tired when I came in, but this was not like me. Even when I was tired, I still handled my business, but on that day I could not. I told Angela I just needed to lie there for a little while longer.

By nightfall, I was still on the floor. Angela came back in the living room and told me I needed to go get in the bed. I told her I was too tired. She walked over to help me up and when she touched me, she said I was burning up with fever. I must have caught a bad cold from somebody at work, and I certainly did not want to give it to my children. When I tried to get up, it took everything I had in me to get to the couch. I knew then, this was more than a bad cold.

I told Angela I needed to go to the hospital. Carl still had not made it home from work, so that meant either calling an ambulance or Angela driving me and taking the kids with us. I did not think I needed an ambulance because the hospital was not far away. Angela called Carl and told him she was taking me to the hospital and that we would have the kids with us.

At the emergency room and I went to triage to get examined. The nurse who was checking me out said my temperature was 104 degrees. The next thing I knew, they were rushing me to the back, taking my clothes off and packing me in ice. I had no idea what was happening to me. They immediately started an intravenous drip line to get some medications and fluids in my body. I fell asleep and when I woke up, I was not sure how long I had been there. It only took me a few minutes to realize that I was in a hospital room and not in the emergency area anymore.

A nurse came in, and told me I was real sick. I asked her how long I had been here and she said two days. I asked her what was wrong with me, but she said I needed to talk to my doctor. I knew it must be serious if she would not tell me. That made me nervous. All kinds of thoughts were going through my head. Did I have cancer, AIDS, or something just as bad? I was scared and alone.

I called my apartment and Angela answered. I asked her if she could call my job and tell them I was in the hospital and she said she already did. As I was talking to her, the doctor came in, so I got off the phone. He went through all the formalities of introducing himself and asking how I was doing. I did not want to be rude, but I really did not care at that moment what his name was, and he already knew how I was doing. I asked him what was wrong with me.

He said I had an infection in my blood, a condition called sepsis. I was relieved to know it was not cancer or AIDS, but it still sounded really serious. I asked him how I got it. He said it looked like I had a bladder infection that turned into a kidney infection and with both gone untreated, the infection had spilled over into my bloodstream. He said it was unusual for that to happen.

He asked if I had been in any pain the last couple of weeks. I told him no. He said for some reason my body never registered the pain, and I should not have been able to walk around and function normally once the bladder infection turned into a kidney infection. It would have been too painful for me not to seek medical attention. I was also dehydrated and came to the hospital just in time.

He said they would get me back to normal and I would be able to go home in a few days. After he left, the nurse came back in. She told me I was lucky to be alive, because sepsis was a very serious and sometimes deadly infection. She said she had been praying for me. I told her thanks, even though she did not realize those were wasted prayers, because I knew that God did not care about me. I wanted Him to, but He just did not. I had tried going to Angela's church in Brownwood. I figured if God helped her get off drugs, then he could help me with my problems. God did not help me; I guess I had done too much wrong in my life.

When I got home, the recovery period was hard. The process actually was a reverse action of what had happened to my body. They flushed the infection out of my bloodstream. Next, they flushed it out of my kidneys and then out of my bladder. I may not have been in pain when I was getting sick, but I sure was in pain now, trying to get all the infection out of my body. The doctor said that was a good sign because it meant that my body was registering pain like it was supposed to. I was in so much pain that I could not even hold my little girl. It even hurt when my son hugged me, but I could not bring myself to tell him that, so I just let him hug me and endured the pain while I went through the recovery process.

In the meantime, Angela was able to get her own place, so she moved out and I would take the children to her every day. It was less convenient, but I never expected for her to stay with us forever, so it did not come as a surprise.

Over the next couple of years, all my brothers and my youngest sister moved to Texas. As each one visited, they decided they wanted to stay. They would come and then return to Brownwood. After they would get back to Brownwood, they would make the decision to live in Texas. Eventually, we were all living in Texas, even my brother Joseph, who went to live with his aunt as a small boy. I would never have imagined that that happening when I first moved away from Brownwood.

A LITTLE OVER TWO and half years after my daughter was born, Carl told me that my sister Jocelyn had been joking around, saying that her daughters were his children. My mind was having trouble comprehending what he had said, so I told him to repeat it. He said it again, using the exact same words. I saw nothing funny about it and told him so. I immediately picked up the phone and called her and asked her about this "joke". When I called her she said it was true and it was not a joke. She said it so casually that you would have thought I was asking her if it was true that two plus two is four. No apology, no words of remorse, just yes, it is true.

I think my mind went blank for a second while the words were processing in my head. After they processed, I cursed her out real good and then hung up the phone. I was so mad that I felt like those cartoon characters that get so mad that you see the smoke coming from their ears and their face turns beet red. If I had been a cartoon character, that is what Carl would have seen right then. I began screaming at him.

I was experiencing so many emotions at one time. I was angry, sad, confused and in disbelief. How could this be happening? Jocelyn was not just my sister, she was my best friend. I had shared so much with her. I talked to her more than anybody else. It never dawned on me not to trust her, especially after all the times I had been there for her and thought she was there for me.

I knew Carl had cheated on me a lot, but never in my wildest dreams would I have thought he would cross the line to cheat on me with my sister! Not only did he cheat with her, but they had kids together?!? My nieces, the children that I helped to raise the first couple years of their lives, were his children. My children's first cousins were their sisters?!? When did this happen? How could this have happened and I not know it? How could Jocelyn do this to me? She never showed any signs that she and Carl had ever been anything more to each other than brother and sister-in-law. Even when we were her foster parents, they were still like sister and brother.

Carl was saying something to me, but I could not hear him because my own thoughts were so loud in my head. He was asking me if I was okay.

Okay? How could I be okay? Would he be okay if he were me? Of course not! Surely he did not think he could just tell me something like that, have Jocelyn confirm that it was true and then we move on like some Lifetime movie just went off.

I asked him if it was true. His response to me did not make any sense. He said if it was true, but he was not saying it was true, it was a long time ago. I looked at him like he was crazy. Either it was true or it was not. Did he think it would not matter to me because it was a long time ago? Was he trying to play with my head? It was not a long time ago to me, because I was just finding out, so as far as I was concerned it was happening right now.

I knew he was lying but I wanted to hear him say he had done it. I was not sure whether or not my nieces were his children, but it would still mean that he had sex with her. He had betrayed me and his brother, and she had betrayed me and her fiancé.

It might sound crazy, but I was angrier at Jocelyn than Carl. She was not only my sister; she was my best friend. I was used to him betraying me, but I never would have thought in a million years that she would betray me. How did she look me in the face, smiling and laughing all those years, knowing what she had done? Why did she even come to Texas?

I could not begin to explain the pain I felt. My pain quickly turned to hatred. She was the one person in the world that I just knew was in my corner. I wanted to know what went through her head every time they slept together and then she listened to me talk about him. How could she have watched how he treated me and then lay down with him? I could not stop all the questions that were running through my mind. I had done some horrible things in my life and hurt a lot of people along the way, but sleeping with your sister/best friend's husband--that was stooping to an all-time low.

The old Josette that used to fight all the time had come out in me again. I wanted to jump Jocelyn and hurt her bad. I wanted to jump Carl also, but he was so much bigger than me. I was going to have to use something other than my hands to hurt him. I just had to figure it out, but somebody was going to pay a heavy price for this, and I knew just the two some-bodies. They were going to be sorry they ever did this to me. They had taken betrayal to a whole new level for me. If I had a gun, I would feel so much better at this moment by shooting Carl.

Carl was trying to talk to me and act like he is clueless. He was asking questions, like he was wondering what Jocelyn was trying to do to us. He said he thought she was jealous and was trying to break us up. I rolled my eyes at him and told him to shut up. He better not even think about putting his hands on me. I was not taking it anymore. He would die tonight if he does. I had no more patience for him.

I think Carl realized that I was in no mood to take his mess. He said he was going to cook dinner. He did not do that often and I surely was not going to eat anything he made. I was steaming mad, so I called Jocelyn back. I wanted to know the answers to my questions. She had better tell me something good, too. I was not sure what that would be that could justify her actions, but I wanted to know something.

Jocelyn was not able to give me any answers. All she could say was she did not know why she did it and that she did not mean to hurt me. What other way would something like this make me feel? I asked her why she did not tell me herself a long time ago. She said it was just never the right time, and then when we broke up she was planning on telling me but never did. I asked her how she could let me go back to him knowing all of this, and all she said was she did not know. For the first time in my life I felt hatred towards her. I screamed at her until I ran out of things to say and then slammed down the phone.

Now Carl was saying he has never slept with her. He wanted me to believe him. He said that I should trust him because I was his wife. Trust?!? Was he for real? I did not trust him farther than I could throw him, and I knew I could not even pick him up. I did not know how he could even let that come out of his mouth. His charm that once worked on me no longer had any effect now.

I told him if it was not true, then he would not have a problem taking a blood test. He said he did not want to do that because it would be an invasion of privacy. Surely he did not realize how stupid he sounded right then. I told him if he did not have a blood test then I was divorcing him for sure, because if his family meant anything to him, he would do it. He finally said he would take the test.

The blood test was scheduled, but Carl never showed up. I had not even told Jocelyn about it. My plan was for him to take his and then have her take my nieces to get tested. He said he could not bring himself to go against his principles. Now he wanted to get principles? Yeah, right. He was such a liar!

I HAD FILED FOR divorce. I had not talked to Jocelyn since this whole thing came out and I asked her about it. I had nothing to say to her. My family did not understand my anger towards her. They felt I should only be mad at Carl. Their opinion did not change the way I felt. She still had not given me a good explanation for why she did it. Not that it would have mattered anyway, but I did want to know why she did it. This difference of opinion caused a big rift in an already strained family relationship. Now everybody was angry at me because I did not want to deal with my sister. How could they not understand?

This was hurting me so bad, yet they wanted me to pretend like it did not. I could not. I did not even want to look at her, let alone be around her. I did not want to pretend anymore like I was okay when things bothered me. I had been angry most of my life about so many things. That anger had always been displaced toward people who had not hurt me and toward me. This time, I was ready to direct my anger where it belonged.

Angela said I was not being rational about this whole thing. She said I was in denial because I still picked up my nieces. Even though I did not want to see or talk to Jocelyn, I loved my nieces. They had not done anything to me. They were like my other children. Angela did not seem to understand this. I understood what it felt like to be an innocent child in the middle of a bad situation, and this was definitely a bad situation. They knew something was wrong, and I did not want them to think it was their fault. They did not ask to be born.

It had been two months since I filed for divorce. Carl had been fighting me on the details every step of the way. Before all this happened, I was in the process of building a house. It was only in my name so I figured I had a plan for living arrangements after the divorce was finalized. Carl had a plan in mind, too. Texas is a community property state, so everything we owned would have been split evenly. This included the new house. Our divorce could have been a speedy one, but he dragged it out to wait for me to close on the house. He had already let me know that I was going to have to give him half of the value of the house. I made more money than him, so he had also been trying to get alimony factored into the divorce settlement. I hated him. I hated my sister. I hated my life.

Two weeks before I was supposed to close on the house, I got laid off. This could not have been happening--what else could have gone wrong? How was I supposed to close on my house if I did not have a job? How was I going to take care of my kids? It was like I was in a downward spiral. I did not tell Carl I got laid off, but he found out anyway because they sent my severance package to the house and he opened it. As soon as he realized I did not have a job, he took a different approach to the divorce settlement. Now he wanted both cars and the kids.

I needed to move out of this house we were in. I could not continue to be in the same space as him. I did not know where I was going when I left there. Without a job, it was going to be hard. I had mentioned this to Angela, but she had not offered her place. She said because she was on Section 8, she could not take us in. I did not know what to do, but I knew that at the end of the day, I could only depend on me, so it was nothing new. When push came to shove, I knew how to make it, even if I had to beg, borrow or steal.

Now that I did not have a job, Carl was back to trying to bully me. One day while my nieces were visiting, we were arguing. I had my baby girl in my arms. Right in the middle of our argument, he grabbed me and was holding me up against the wall by my neck. Even though he was squeezing my neck really hard, to the point that I could hardly breathe, I held my daughter really tight. The floor was made of tile and I did not want to drop her on it. He was yelling at me and wanted me to answer him, but I was unable to talk. My son and two nieces were standing off to the side, watching him.

He finally let me go. He started walking across the room really fast. He had on socks and the next thing I knew, he slipped and fell right on his butt. Under any other circumstance, it would have been a funny sight, but laughter was the last thing on my mind. My neck was sore, it felt like if he had kept squeezing he would have broken my wind pipe. I was definitely going to kill him now.

Later in the week, I took my children over to Angela's. I needed to get them out of the house. I was going to kill Carl that night. The pain was too great. I walked around like a robot going through the motions of taking care of my children and trying to find work. I felt like I was going crazy. I could not focus, and it was taking everything in me to keep going each day. The thought of seeing him die consumed me. I wanted him to feel the pain that he had made me feel.

MY FRIEND SHERRIE, FROM work, had told me that I could stay with her family while I figured things out. I had accepted her offer. I did not tell her about my plan to kill Carl. While I was waiting for him to come back to the house, I was boxing up some of my son's things. Next, I started packing a few of my daughter's things. As I was standing in her closet, the thought of killing Carl when he got home was overwhelming. I was going to kill my sister, too. They deserved it. I did not want to face people after they found out what happened between him and my sister. How could I explain that and it make sense to them? I was thinking of all the shame and embarrassment that I would feel over and over again.

I felt like my brain was about to explode; it was too much for me. I reached up to take some more clothes out of my daughter's closet, and I collapsed to the floor in tears. I was emotionally drained and I knew that I had hit rock bottom. I did not know why, but I cried out to God and told Him if He was real then I needed Him to help me.

The next thing I knew, I had this vision of me in a white jumpsuit sitting at a picnic style table and my children were sitting across from me. I realized God was showing me the outcome of what I was getting ready to do. I had already thought about prison being a possibility so that did not get to me. I was willing to risk prison for the relief of seeing both of them dead.

What got to me was seeing my children in the vision. If I killed Carl and went to prison, my children would become foster children. I was getting ready to put their lives on the same course that my life, Angela's life and her mother's life had gone. It would have been another generation of foster children. I could not let that happen. I began to thank God for showing me life beyond my emotions. He knew exactly what to show me to get my attention. That was the first time that I knew that God was truly concerned about me and heard my cry. When Carl got home, he had no idea that God had just saved his life.

I could go on now. I was not going to kill Carl or my sister. I packed up a few more things for my daughter and grabbed a few things for myself. The kids and I were living in Sherrie's den and sleeping on her pull-out sofa bed. I cried at night, thinking about what my life had become. I had no home of my own and two innocent children depending on me.

During the day, I dropped them off with Angela and pretended everything was okay. There was a smile on my lips that never reached my eyes. I needed God's help again. I needed a job and a place to stay. I tried praying but I did not have the right words to say, so I just said what was on my mind. If anyone were listening, they would have thought that someone was in the room with me.

The kids and I had been at Sherrie's house for two weeks. I was going to try to get an apartment. I was hoping I would get a job soon so that the rent would not be a problem. I would use my severance package for the first two months. After I filled out the application, the lady told me that they had a special going and the first three months of rent would be free. I kept my cool on the outside, but on the inside I was leaping for joy. It was just what I needed. Their three months plus my two months would definitely be more than enough to cover me. I was wondering in the back of my mind if God made this happen, so I said a quiet *thank you God*, just in case.

I got approved for the apartment and she gave

me my key right then and there. What a relief. I told Sherrie I had found a place and the kids and I would move out the next day. I told her I would be forever grateful she was there when I had no place to go.

After moving in to my new apartment, I went to get the rest of my things. When I got to the house, Carl had thrown most of my things in the middle of the kitchen floor. Anything that was really worth keeping had been destroyed. I had bought a full length mink coat when I was in Brownwood and it was gone. He had also taken my laptop. Now, the only clothes that I had were the ones I had originally taken with me when I went to Sherrie's house.

Trying to get my furniture and my other belongings out of the house proved to be quite an ordeal. Carl would show up to the house every time I had arranged for someone to help me move my things out. I think he was always somewhere nearby watching the house. He had taken everything he wanted out of the house and then called the police to tell them I was illegally taking things out.

With our divorce not finalized, the police told me I could not take anything until we had a final settlement. They did not care that he had already taken things out. They said they could not do anything about that and they could only go by the court order. The good thing about the police being there was that they took record of the major items in the house and told Carl he could not take anything else out of the house. Once I knew he could not take anything else, I was able to peacefully wait until the court settlement to get my things. I was just happy to be away from him.

I HAD BEEN IN my apartment for three months and I had not found work yet. I really needed God to hear me again. I had started going to church again. I did not go every Sunday, but I tried to make it sometimes. A friend of mine in Brownwood called me every Sunday afternoon to find out if I went to church. Whenever I told him I did not go, he would encourage me to go the next Sunday. I was definitely hit or miss on Sundays, but at least I was going. I had also started reading my Bible on occasion. I was not waiting for an invitation anymore so I could get the green light to have Bible Study.

I ended up living in that apartment for eight months. After about five months of being there, I was contacted by the builder of the company that I had tried to build a house with. He asked if I wanted them to build me another house. I explained to him that I had not found work, so I was not in a position to do that. He told me they only had one lot left in the subdivision I had been trying to move into. I told him I appreciated him thinking about me, but I could not at that time. He was very persistent. I finally gave him the excuse that if the lot had been across the street, I would have done it. I liked that one better. He said okay and we got off the phone. He was a painful reminder of what once had almost been. I had never owned a house before and I had been so close. In reality, I knew that it was good that things turned out the way they did, because I would have more legal troubles with Carl trying to gain from it financially.

About an hour later the builder called me back excitedly and said the lot I wanted was available. He said the people who had it, called and said they wanted to switch lots. I had run out of excuses. I had already told him I did not have a job and did not know when I would get one. He said he had confidence that I would get one and that I had nothing to lose by them building it. When I did not close on the other house, they kept my earnest money, per the agreement. For whatever reason, instead of making a profit from it, he wanted to take that same money and try again. I knew it was out of the kindness of his heart, because he was not obligated to do so. I finally said yes. He was right; what did I have to lose?

While the house was being built, I was busy

looking for work. If I could just find a job, this could become a reality. Every job turned up as a dead end. This was the year after the terrorist attacks that brought down the Twin Towers in New York City. The economy had taken a downturn, and I was one of the many that was affected by it.

When the house was complete, I still had not found work. The builder encouraged me to keep looking and said that it was my house. He said he was not selling it to anyone but me. I had hit so many obstacles during this time that I wanted to give up. I did not understand why he was being so nice to me. The house was beautiful and I was sure it could sell easily.

I had started attending Evangelism classes at church. I wanted to do something out of appreciation for what God had done for me, but I already knew that I did not want to sing in the choir or serve on the usher board. On my first night of class, I realized I had gotten in over my head. These were important people in the church, not a nobody like me. They were ministers, deacons, or some other title in the church. The instructor asked everybody to tell why they were there. As he went around the room, almost all of them said they had been called. I was the last to answer. I told him that I did not get a phone call, but had responded to a yellow flyer that was in my church program, the kind that are given out on Sundays so that the congregation can follow the order of service.

I immediately knew I had said something wrong based on the looks on the other people in the class. I just did not know what. The instructor told me that there had not been any flyers put in the church programs. I thought that must have been why everybody was looking at me, but I knew that I had a flyer in mine. I even described it to them. Later, I found out it was not the church program comment that made the class look at me strangely. When the others said they had been called, they were not talking about a phone call. They were making reference to the scripture in Matthew chapter 22 verse 14, in the Bible that says for many are called, but few are chosen (KJV). I felt like such an idiot when I found out.

I HAD FINALLY FOUND employment! Well, I had a letter of intent for employment. I would not start for another three weeks, when the position was actually available. I called the mortgage company and let them know. They said they would move forward with the letter of intent. I had a long job history and this was in the same field, so they felt comfortable with it.

One the day of my closing, I sat in the title company nervously. My mortgage loan officer and realtor were there. They were a husband and wife team who had helped me every step of the way. He was a loan officer and she was a realtor. They said I had nothing to worry about at this point, because once you made it to the closing it was just a matter of signing the papers. After we were called to the back, they told us the bank had put a condition on the closing. I did not know what that meant. He explained that it meant they were not releasing the funds.

I knew it was too good to be true. I had not

started work yet and my credit was not that good. I guess it was time to wake up from this dream of buying a house. I was trying to keep my composure, but a few tears kept falling from my eyes. The title officer said that since we were already there, I might as well sign the papers. My loan officer was on the phone, trying to find out what the problem was. After all the papers were signed, it was time to go. We had not heard back from the bank. Normally, from what the title officer said, I would have received the keys to my house after I had signed everything. Unfortunately for me, I was leaving empty-handed. My loan officer said that he would keep trying to get through to the bank.

It was raining really hard when we left the title company. That worked perfectly for me, because the rain helped to mask the downpour of tears I was shedding. I cried all the way back to my apartment. I asked myself what I was thinking, trying to build a house without a job. When I got inside my apartment, I fell to my knees right in the middle of the living room. I told God that if He let me have the house, I would serve Him with my whole heart for the rest of my life. I really meant it. I was not trying to bargain with God using some empty promise. He had already helped me out so much this year that I knew for a fact that He was real and I could trust Him. There was nothing I could do, but I had begun to believe that God could do everything.

Almost one hour later, my phone rang and it was the realtor. He said the bank had waived the condition on the closing! I could not believe what I was hearing. He said I could pick up my keys the next day. I told him thank you and got off the phone. I started jumping around and screaming at the top of my lungs, "Thank YOU, God!" The tears were still flowing down my face, but now they were tears of joy. Other than the birth of my children, this was the most amazing thing that had ever happened to me.

I managed to complete Evangelism training. It was not an easy task learning how to study the Bible on a regular basis and speak to an audience. I graduated at the top of my class. I really amazed myself with that accomplishment because I just wanted to finish the class and trying to be at the head of the class was not even on my radar. I realized that the more I read the Bible, the more I was changing for the better. I could feel the change. I did not want to do a lot of the things I used to do and I was not cursing all the time. I even bought a gospel CD for the first time in my life.

IT SEEMED LIKE FOR the last few Sundays the message had been on forgiveness. I tried to ignore it, but it kept eating at me. I had already told Jocelyn that I forgave her, and I forgave Carl, also. When I really thought about it, I knew that I had not truly forgiven Jocelyn, because she never told me why she had slept with Carl. Whenever she was around, I could barely look at her. The more the message on unforgiveness was preached, the more I had to be honest with myself that I was still hurting and needed to forgive her from my heart and not just with my words.

I wish I could say that I did it immediately after I knew that I needed to, but I did not. My pride and stubbornness was in the way. There was a guest minister one Sunday and his message was on forgiveness. Not forgiveness of one man to another, but the forgiveness we have received from God. With all the wrong things that I have done in my life, including saying God never helped me and I had done it all by myself, God still forgave me. He had forgiven me before I even asked for the forgiveness; I just had to receive it by accepting His son Jesus Christ as my Lord and Savior.

This message made me shed tears. Who was I to not forgive my sister for what she had done? In God's eyes, her sin was no greater than mine. I had been holding her hostage with my unforgiveness and little did I know I was keeping myself bound, also. I called Jocelyn and asked her to forgive me for not truly forgiving her. Then I told her that I forgave her for what she had done and that I did not need to hear her reasons for doing what she did, because that no longer mattered. I told her that I loved her and I would not make her feel uncomfortable being around me ever again. She accepted my apology and asked me to forgive her. I could not explain the weight that was lifted off me in that very moment. I knew the reason I finally forgave her for real was because God had healed my broken heart, so I was able to do it.

ONE DAY ANGELA CALLED and said she needed to come over. I started to tell her I did not want her to because I was busy enjoying my day off, but she said it was a matter of her life or death. She can be really dramatic sometimes. When she got there, we sat in my living room so we could talk.

She told me she wanted to ask my forgiveness, because she had been angry and bitter at me. That surprised me. I had no idea she felt that way. Now I was curious to hear what she had to say. She told me it was time for me to forgive her and to stop holding her past over her. I told her I was not holding her past over her. She asked me to let her finish, so I shut up.

She began to tell me how I could not go far in ministry until I forgave her, because I would not be able to minister to people like her. She also told me she loved me and that I was rejecting her. She also wanted me to know how much my brothers and sisters loved me. I knew I said I would be quiet and listen, but I had to stop her right then, before she went too much further.

I told her how from a child up until now I had never felt love from her. She was not there to talk to me and give me direction. She was not there when I needed her to teach me how to care for myself or love myself. I just wanted to know what it felt like to have someone love me and think I was beautiful. I told her I never even knew what love was until God was in my life. When I really gave my life to God, I learned what love was, because God is love. It was after that, that I could really love myself. I could also then love others. I learned I did not know how to love Carl or understand that he did not know how to love me back. Without God, I would have still been in that black hole, searching for something but not really knowing what that something was.

I was crying at this point because all those things that were inside of me were sitting right there at the top, ready to come out. I told her I did not understand how she could sit there and judge me, telling me how much my brothers and sisters loved and missed me and that I had turned my back on everyone. I told her that other than one of my twin brothers and Joseph, nobody called me.

I had called everyone and left messages, yet they did not call me back.

I even shared with her how I finally truly forgave Jocelyn and even asked her to forgive me for having waited so long to do it. I told her how I forgave my youngest sister for the $900 she owed me yet refused to pay back and how I told her to consider it a blessing because God had blessed me. I decided I was not going to let money come between us. That was definitely a true heart change, because I did not have $900 to just give away. I could have used the money especially since it was during the time I was laid off. But I had to come understand that God had maintained and sustained me over the years, so I did not have to rely upon a person to do it. But even with that, my sister did not call me.

And the final things I needed to get off my chest was how after all the years of me looking out for everybody else when I could financially and never asking for anything in return, when I was laid off for six months, none of them tried to see if I needed anything for my children. I reminded her of how when I took her out to eat on her birthday, I asked how she and everybody else were doing. She gave me updates, one by one. She then asked how my children were doing. I told her that she never once asked me how I was doing or what was going on with me. I needed her to know that I noticed that she always hugged my kids, but never me. I told her she had been a great grandmother, but not a good mother for me, but I learned how to forgive her. I knew it was a lot, but it was time for me to say what I felt.

She stood up right in the middle of my talking so she could hug me, but I asked her to sit back down. She started saying how much she loved me. She said she did not know what I was expecting from her. All I was thinking was how sad that was, because for me it only confirmed what I felt had known for some time: she did not know me. She finally finished what she had to say and stood up. I stood up, too. She hugged me really hard and told me from now on she would hug me every time she saw me. I did not want to hurt her feelings, but I half-heartedly hugged her back because of my fear of still being rejected by her. I had forgiven her but knew it would take time to develop a relationship, and I did not want to pretend anymore with my feelings.

When I stopped letting my forgiveness be wrapped in my fear, I was able to stop thinking of her as Angela and start thinking of her as Mom. Perfect love casts out all fear. I John chapter 4 verse 18 (KJV). That was a tough one for me, also. I did not share this with her; I just started doing it, because she did not know that she had just been Angela and not Mom to me all these years.

THERE HAVE BEEN MANY challenges since that day I first cried out to God, but he has brought me through them all. I was engaged for a period of time after my divorce, but I called off the wedding. I realized I was going to marry someone who had reservations about being married. I wanted a husband who knew without question he wanted to spend his life with me. I wanted a man who was not afraid to leave behind everything to make me his bride and our motive for being married would be love until death do us part.

There were some who felt I had blown my only chance to be married again when I called it off, but it was that kind of desperate thinking that made me marry Carl. This time I wanted to trust God, and I knew that was what I was supposed to. I was not that desperate young lady who was suffering from low self-esteem anymore. I knew that I was beautiful, valued, loved and fearfully and wonderfully made by God.

After all I have been through, I know that

God desires for all people to be whole and saved regardless of what they may have done. The stripes that Jesus took on His way to Calvary were not just for our physical healing but for those emotionally wounded, dark places. I was wounded in darkness but Jesus brought me into His marvelous light, where I was healed.

There were some people that said they found parts of my testimony offensive because they said I would tell it as if I was proud of what I have done. I am not proud of the things that I did in my life, but I am comforted in knowing that there is now no condemnation in what I did because I am in Christ Jesus. Once God forgives you, you have to forgive yourself and others and move on with your life. You have to be strong enough not to let anyone tear you down or make you feel bad for what you have done. You see, when I tell my testimony about the days when my life was so dark, it is now like it happened to someone else and I am just sharing their story--and in part that would be true, because I am a new creature in Christ and those old things have passed away. All things have become new in my life. 2 Corinthians chapter 5 verse 17.

I refuse to be imprisoned ever again by my past sins. I can tell the truth of my testimony and the truth has made me free. In the words of the late, great Dr. Martin Luther King, "Free at last, free at last. Thank God Almighty, I am free at last"! The Bible puts it this way: if the Son makes you free, you shall be free indeed. John chapter 8 verse 36 (KJV).

We all need help sometimes. I realize now Angela needed help being a mom. In my younger years, God gave me the strength and capacity to step in for her. I was angry and resentful about it for a long time because I did not understand, but now I do. I understand that I had a purpose then and I have a purpose now. God's plans for me are sure and good, and He will bring them to pass.

Despite having been a liar, a thief, angry, bitter, unforgiving, selfish, promiscuous and having attempted suicide, God still loved me before I loved myself. His love for people is so great. It is a love so great that it truly cannot be comprehended. He was with me, even when I was not with Him. Every time I thought I was all alone, God was right there with me, and He is right there with you.

No matter what you may be going through in life, you have to believe that God made you with purpose. He loves you in spite of whatever you have done and will do. It may be that you were betrayed, hurt badly or have low self-esteem, or maybe you were the one that betrayed and hurt people. If you have used your body in the wrong way or allowed others to use your body in the wrong way, God is waiting to cleanse you and purify you. Maybe you tried to or have been thinking about committing suicide. Do not think about that anymore. God wants you to live and not die.

You no longer have to go looking for love in all the wrong places, hoping that you will find it. There is one waiting to love you beyond your wildest dreams, one standing by to give you comfort and give you peace. He is the creator, God Almighty. There is no love greater than the love of God. His love teaches us how to give and receive love to our fullest capacity.

God does not reject anyone that desires to receive His love, His attention or His acceptance. If you believe that Jesus Christ is the Son of God and died and rose for your sins, all you have to do is ask Him to come into your heart and forgive you for your sins. I spent many years desiring a father, and I had one all along. God says in Psalm chapter 68 verse 5, that He is a father of the fatherless (KJV). He wants to take care of you.

When man says no but God says yes, there is nothing that can stop you but you. I did not always know or believe this, but looking back over my life, I have seen it to be so. I want to motivate you to move past any negativity and self-destruction that may be present in your life. If you can do that, then success can be a reality, and not even the sky will be able to limit you. There are no limits on God when you are following the path that He has already prepared for you. Do not look at your current circumstances; look at God. Your circumstances might say you cannot, but God says you can. The army has a slogan that says be all that you can be, but I say be all that God says He created you to be. He has declared in 1st Peter chapter 2 verse 9 that you are a royal priest, a holy nation, God's very own possession. As a result, you can show others the goodness of God, for he called you out of the darkness into his wonderful light (NLT).

When you know who you are, you do not have to be what others say you will be, when it does not line up with God's word. It does not matter what it looks like now, it only matters what God has said. You are royalty, see yourself as just that. Carl and others were able to treat me the way they did because I did not know that I was royalty. I could hate myself because I did not know I was loved. I could not see my own beauty because I was waiting for others to tell me I was beautiful. I acted like a cubic zirconia instead of the precious diamond God made me.

A cubic zirconia is costume jewelry, and I had worn a costume and mask for too long and lived as if I did not have any real value. I would have a smile on my lips that rarely reached my eyes. I now know my worth and I pray you now know yours. It is time to get all the coal cleaned off you so that you can sparkle too like the beautiful jewel you are.

Many wrote me off as hopeless and I felt helpless. Despite everything, I have come to realize that it is not how you start the fight, it is how you finish. Sometimes you do not have people on the sidelines cheering you on, but you cannot finish the fight unless you get in it and stay in it. I want to encourage and inspire you to get in the fight.

When things in life are beating you up, whether it is a broken heart, a lost job, finances or whatever it may be, do not throw in the towel. You may feel like the opponent is just too big for you to fight anymore but just like a professional boxer, you may have to go to your corner, where the Holy Spirit who is your trainer, will encourage you to stay in the fight.

He will re-assure you that you will win, because Jesus has already guaranteed you the victory. He will remind you that God is on your side and He is the one who is really fighting the fight, you just need to stand in the ring as a representative. He knows your enemy and his fighting technique.

It may seem like it's all over and when it feels like you cannot take any more blows of life, God comes in and knocks your enemy right out. But just like the professional fighter, if you do not get in the ring and stay in the fight, you will never win. So I say to you again, do not throw in the towel!

You may find that your towel has a lot of blood on it, but do not worry; it is not your blood but the blood of Jesus that was shed for you. It is a fixed fight against satan that Jesus has already won for us. Romans chapter 8 verse 37 says you are more than a conqueror!

I am no longer afraid to stand boldly before people to tell them that even though I was wounded in the darkness of sin, I have been healed in the light. I want you to be able to stand and do the same.

I hope the tale of my journey has helped your journey. If you are not in darkness, I am sure you know someone that is. Share the love and light of God, so that they also can stop being wounded in darkness and get healed in the light.

My Prayer for you…

Dear Heavenly Father, I pray that the reader of this book has confessed their sins to you and have received you as their Lord and Savior. I thank you now that they shall have peace that passes all understanding. I thank you that by Jesus' stripes they are already healed in their body, mind and emotions. I speak to every dark place, every wounded place, every bitter memory, every lie that the devil has made them believe and I call forth your light to expose the darkness, your healing to mend the wounded places and your word of truth to expose the lies they have been told. I ask that you increase their faith so that they can walk out their healing. I pray that you guide them and lead them in the path of righteousness for your name's sake. I thank you that they can rest assured that you will never leave them nor forsake them and that you have a good plan for them. I thank you now that they have chosen life over death and that they will have life more abundantly. I thank you because I know that you are faithful and will be with them. I thank you and bless for you being almighty God, our creator, the Alpha and the Omega, the beginning and the end, the author and finisher of our faith. I love you and thank you that they are blessed. In Jesus' name I pray, Amen.

God bless you!

Eye hath not seen, nor ear heard, neither have

entered into the heart of man, the things which God hath prepared for them that love him. 1 Corinthians 2:9

Contacting the Author

To contact LaTonya G. Green directly regarding
speaking engagements or comments on the book:

www.latonyagreen.com

via **email**:
healedinthelight@yahoo.com